LOVING LUDDY

A Novel

Homer Dowdy

LION
PUBLISHING

Lion Publishing
A Division of Cook Communications
4050 Lee Vance View
Colorado Springs, CO 80918, USA

Cover design by Bill Gray
Cover illustration by Kevin Beilfuss

First printing, 1997
Printed in the United States of America
01 00 99 98 97 5 4 3 2 1

Dowdy, Homer E.
Loving Luddy / Homer Dowdy.
p. cm.
ISBN 0-7459-3762-4
I. Title.
PS3554.09315L68 1997 97-7658
813'.54-dc21 CIP

To Nancy,
my wonderful wife
of fifty years

Chapter One

Luddy Newton, sometimes called Fig, was nominated from the floor for deacon at a special meeting of the church. Ordinarily, the members would have laughed and considered the one proposing him as a jokester, but the two candidates put forward by the nominating committee had over the last two weeks fallen out of favor with a lot of folk and Luddy was elected, only about ten votes shy of being their unanimous choice.

People were mad at Weldon Basker and Bob Franklin because the two men were mad at each other, and the little feud that was growing up over their differences seemed to be of the infectious type.

"Why, with the strife that's undercurrent in this church," fumed Harry Churtle at the meeting called to fill a single vacancy on the church's governing body, "I reckon we could do worse than make Luddy Newton, black eye and all, our new deacon."

"I second the nomination," came a ringing voice from somewhere in the middle of the seventy or so members all huddled on one side of the sanctuary.

"Well, I didn't exactly first it, but on second thought, I think I will," said Harry. "I nominate Luddy Newton."

"Hmmm," mused Gilroy McAfee, the solemn chairman of the deacons, who always strove to be fair at any meeting he presided over and, to the best of his acquaintance with *Robert's Rules*, to conduct it strictly according to that gentleman's determinations. "We have a nomination from the floor, and a second—although the second came first. Any other nominations, fore or aft?"

He paused five seconds. "Hearing none, we will vote."

The quarrel between Weldon Basker and Bob Franklin was said to be a high-level contention over doctrine, but everyone knew its roots were planted firmly in the middle aisle of the church's three aisles, and in the fact that by tradition only one of the three ushers trod that central passageway while passing the collection plates Sunday morning and evening. The position of middle usher, considered the superior of his two associates, each of whom worked from the side aisles next to the windows, rotated every three years among the three.

"You've had it three years," Bob said to Weldon one Sunday as they pinned on their plastic carnations and practiced their welcoming smiles. "Now it's my turn."

"No, two years. One year yet to go."

"Three."

"Two."

"Three."

"Two. I started the week after I got my new teeth." They showed now, for Weldon had not lost his smile.

"That was three years ago. I know. You were at my house for a Valentine's party of the adult Bible class, and you'd just got your new teeth. That was the night my canary died."

"Are you insinuating—"

This led to a glowering dispute over which should prevail—the "judge not" of Matthew 7, or Paul's admonition to the Corinthians that they count one of their number worthy of expulsion.

Weldon was a former deacon. He had served three two-year terms which, according to the bylaws, was the limit until after a year's sabbatical. He would have been nominated earlier to serve again, but Mrs. Basker still presided over the Women's Missionary Society and their daughter Claire was president of the youth group, so there was considerable sentiment that Weldon should wait a year until Rebecca retired to the Society's sidelines and Claire went off to college. This current year would have been Weldon's without question, except the nominating committee confounded things by throwing Bob Franklin up against him.

Bob, a middle-aged pillar of the church like Weldon, had once been its treasurer. He had handled the finances well, with no breath of scandal or hint of slipshod work. His company had sent him away to Cleveland for a year, so he had rendered up the books to Ray Kittle. When Bob returned there was no compelling reason to change back, so now for five years Ray had been treasurer. But all this time a lot of the members thought Bob was deserving of something besides ushering, and if he couldn't be treasurer, perhaps he might be elected a deacon.

At first it appeared there would be a fair contest, with even the two candidates broadcasting good-naturedly, "Let the best man win." Until one evening Bob's wife asked rather off-handedly if it wasn't about their turn to host the Valentine's party again.

"How long since we had it?" Bob asked.

"This will be the third year," Eleanor replied. "Us, then Bessie McAfee, then the Kittles. Now with February coming on fast, somebody should do some planning, and it looks like it might be up to us."

Ellie's thoughts were of heart-shaped cakes and pretty lace and flowers and games middle-aged folk liked to play as if they were youngsters again. Bob's mind went back to that last party in their home, back to Weldon's new teeth, and his subsequent assumption of the head usher's post. Sweeping ahead, he focused on how it would be for him, Bob Franklin, to serve as pivot usher and to effortlessly juggle four plates, two on each side of the aisle. Perhaps he'd be a little ragged for a Sunday or two, but the Reverend Barrett, looking down from his pastoral chair on the platform, the choir from its loft, and the full congregation from where they sat, would soon see that he was as skilled as his predecessors—particularly his immediate predecessor. And if he sneezed, as he seldom had to do, he wouldn't make a big production of it like the present chief usher always did, bending over, dropping whatever was in hand, and causing people to think he may have suffered a heart attack.

On the Sunday that followed Ellie's question, Bob spoke to Weldon about the rotation.

"I don't see how a person flouting established doctrine can serve as a deacon of this church," Weldon said over the next two weeks to anyone who might be a member in good standing and above the minimum age for voting in the business meeting. "'Judge not'—it's very clear. A scriptural injunction. And that's what Bob is doing to me. He judges me as unfit to continue in the responsibility I've tried to faithfully discharge over these past two years."

"To lie is to break one of the commandments," Bob said on other occasions to the same people. "And to covet is another."

"Covet? Who's coveting?"

"Well, certainly not me. I only want to see the written and unwritten laws of this church carried out. If *he* covets a position that prevailing practice says he's no longer entitled to, well, isn't he that brother which the Apostle Paul says should be put out, not continued as head usher under false pretenses, and certainly not elected as deacon?"

They carried on their quarrel mostly through third parties, but at a church supper in the basement a week before the deacon vacancy was to be filled, the two adversaries squared off in a direct verbal assault. While the women of the congregation put the last of the hot food on the tables, the men lingered in their small circles getting in a final word about baseball or politics or a layman's understanding of theology. In one such group Weldon Basker and Bob Franklin argued, while Luddy Newton, his friend Harry Churtle, and one or two others stood by listening.

"Right here," said Bob, holding open a Bible and thrusting it accusingly toward Weldon, "it speaks straight to the issue with you plainly in mind: 'That the aged men be sober, grave, temperate, sound in faith, in charity, in patience.'"

"And who are you calling aged?" demanded Weldon.

"It's not what *I* call anyone. It's what the Word says. See, 'exhort and rebuke with all authority.'"

"Here, give me that!" cried an exasperated Weldon. He shot out a hand to wrest the Bible from this contentious expositor, and in so doing poked his fist solidly in the eye of the man next to him, who just happened to be rising from tying his shoe. Luddy Newton, knocked off balance, fell into Harry Churtle, buckling him at the knees. This sent Harry flying into the nearby table, upsetting it, and with a shattering crash hurtling dishes, glassware, silverware, and flower vases to the concrete floor and inundating a wide area of the basement with a tidal wave of cole slaw, mashed potatoes and gravy, plates of butter, bowls of green beans, and pitchers of coffee and milk. A few homemade biscuits rolled to a stop just short of the stairs to the vestibule above.

"Armageddon's upon us!" exclaimed one of the cooks, rushing in from the kitchen.

"It will be when we get home," added one of her coworkers. She saw her husband in the group at the hub of destruction and presumed that he, somehow, must naturally be at fault.

The mess was cleaned up, the table righted, and new places set. Food held back for intended seconds was dished up, and in short order the pastor asked the blessing, choosing to overlook the immediate past in his review of the Lord's dealings with them. Soon the hum of a half-hundred or so diners filled the low-ceilinged fellowship hall, but the usual level of gregarious babel was lacking. Luddy's blossoming black eye seemed to symbolize the pall that was beginning to settle on the gathering. It was not so much one camp against another, though some blamed Weldon and some Bob. Rather, the conflict of these two and its debilitating effect had enveloped the members in a sort of general malaise, and none seemed to know a way to shake it.

They had no red meat, so they applied chicken livers to Luddy's swelling eye. Since the giblets were already cooked, they left no effect except the sting of their grease. The group tried singing lively choruses to lighten spirits, but the impromptu song leader was a little heavy with his jokes, some of which a portion of the crowd deemed inappropriate for the occasion. Within a week, however, the mood improved more noticeably than did Luddy's face. No one could explain it, but his election, unlikely as it was, did much to lift the veil. This man who had always been ignored, shunted aside, or regarded as little more than an oddity, had quite mysteriously brought them together. Now they could be unanimous, except for fewer than a dozen holdouts, in chastising not each other, but the two warring ushers.

If Rosewood Fellowship Church had been a large congregation, the tiff between two parishioners no doubt would have been swallowed up in the anonymity of size. But as churches go in the medium cities of mid-America, Rosewood was destined to suffer a lingering indigestion from the bitter dregs of any quarrel among its members. Of some two hundred fifty persons present on any given Sunday morning, many more than half were children, of which the infants and toddlers cooed and cried in a couple of nurseries during the worship service and the kids up to middle-school age were siphoned off into their own Junior Church. Of the seventy-some bodies at the business meeting, about fifty were of voting age. It was a small church, or to phrase it another way, a rather large family, and nothing that was done or said or, at times, even thought, remained under wraps for long.

Rosewood had been started some forty years before, the good Pastor Ernest Thayer its midwife at birth. The Reverend Thayer was officially retired, but the way he interpreted Scripture, the God of the Ages never slacked off, so why, in the short span of a lifetime allotted His servant, should he? Inviting his neighbors into his living room, he started a Bible study for this new, middle-class suburb. People with strong or faint connections to the Baptists, Methodists, or Congregationalists, with a few Presbyterians and Lutherans and some completely unchurched thrown in, assembled each week. Eventually a couple of vacant parcels within the subdivision were purchased, and on this land a small but adequate building was raised.

The church was made to resemble those traditional village temples of New England, though not as grand or classic. An all-white wooden structure, it had a square entrance tower surmounted by a steeple rising some fifteen or twenty feet, its eight tapering sides of black shingles making the spire appear round from ground level—a feature possibly having creedal significance. Crowning it was a white ball, like a cloud the size of a man's hand against the blue sky.

Inside, simplicity reigned. The two sections of pews faced a platform on which centered a lumbering, dark-stained pulpit and, balancing one another, two heavy oak chairs padded with black leather. The choir occupied two rows of seats behind this furniture. To the loft's rear, slightly elevated, stood a baptistery, and above it a stained-glass window of Christ in Gethsemane. It was the only window of color—the three down each outside aisle being comprised of opaque glass in the lower sash and clear in the upper. An upright piano and a small electronic organ completed the sanctuary's accoutrements, except for American and Christian flags standing in the corners backing up the instruments.

Pastor Thayer continued on for quite a few years beyond the Biblical mean. He eventually was laid to rest, however, and in the following years the succession of shepherds to this small flock was more numerous than generally thought healthy for any congregation. The present pastor, the Reverend Peter Barrett, was now in his second year. He, his wife Sheila, and their teenage son, Ryan, appeared to be reasonably happy in their charge, and so appeared their parishioners with them. The Newtons had been among the young families attracted early on to Rosewood Fellowship. People who were around at the time recalled that Claude Newton was dragged to church by his pretty, defenseless-looking but determined wife, Priscilla. For a long while the members looked on Claude as a big, shaggy dog—gruff, domineering and slobberly boorish. He certainly gave no hint of the delicate. Yet after his son was born, he inexplicably changed as he hadn't when two years before Priscilla bore him a daughter.

Claude named the boy Ludlow, after a typesetting machine he worked on in the town's largest print shop. The Ludlow set big-print type for signs in a local supermarket, and Claude loved that machine and his work. The day his son was born he showed up at the hospital with a huge placard bearing the boy's name. He gave the nurse two dollars to prop it on the baby's bassinet so it faced the window through which doting parents and relatives ogled their newborn.

Priscilla thought they should wait a few weeks to have him dedicated to the Lord. Claude said do it now. There was something about the child that fostered an immediacy in the once slow-responding man. Less than two weeks old, little Ludlow was handed from parent to pastor in front of an approving congregation, was caressed and prayed over, and was in process of being handed back when a miscue occurred and the baby dropped in the exchange. He was caught, however, by his father, this physical nimbleness seeming to reflect a rejuvenation in the man's inner self.

The Newtons came to believe that the best way to train children to sit reverently in church was to have them sit in church. So they kept four-year-old Marcia and two-year-old Luddy with them as each Sunday morning they made their way to their usual pew, on the left side a few rows from the front. One Sunday the piano, rather than the organ, accompanied the choir's anthem, and Luddy sat up and noticed that this box just out of his reach produced pleasant sounds like the one at his grandmother's house. Later, as the parents gave rapt attention to the pastor's message, Luddy slipped from his daddy's lap and crawled down the side aisle. Reaching the piano unobserved, he pulled himself up and with the fortissimo of a Van Cliburn banged on the keys, striking every octave from middle C downward.

Startled, the minister broke off in mid-sentence, and his hearers thought he'd stopped to gather in breath for shouting a main point. Between some subsequent scowling and a lot of tittering across the congregation, Pastor Thayer looked around to identify the source of the disturbance, and discovering it said with some relief, "You recall I spoke of Gabriel in my opening illustration. For a moment there, I thought he had crashed through the roof, blowing his horn."

Claude scrambled out of his seat and snatched up the tiny virtuoso. He hustled back down the aisle toward the rear.

"Luddy play panner like Grandma's," said the child in the loud, clear voice of innocence.

His father bent his head low, trying to hide his red face behind his son.

"Give cookie."

"No cookie," Claude rasped in the tot's ear.

"Luddy good boy. Give cookie, Daddy. Give cookie."

Having jangled a few nerves that Sunday, he could be expected to tweak a few more here and there long after graduating from training pants.

The next time his lack of inhibition garnered the attention of the entire assemblage was during the children's Sunday School Christmas pageant. Marcia, now six, Luddy who had turned four, and their baby sister, Leeann, almost three, made up the angel complement—an arrangement by which, being of one family, they could practice their parts at home. On the night of the performance Luddy had difficulty with his halo; it kept slipping down over his eyes. When the production arrived at the point the angels were to say in unison, "Peace on earth, goodwill toward men," the circle of false gold fell to his nose. He grabbed at it, pulling it down around his neck, and above the timid tones of his sisters shouted in full stage voice, "For cryin' out loud, this dang thing don't fit!" Then, instead of wailing as a maddened child would, he laughed at his extreme behavior, and this confused his audience.

"If that was my son," said an aging matron who had borne neither sons nor daughters, "I'd whale the audacity out of the boy." Luddy heard her and though he did not understand which part of his anatomy the lady in the second row would eliminate, he gathered from the curl of her lip that there must be something about him worthy of condemnation.

The halo hardly fit, people agreed, but their judgment sprang from more than a faulty string of tinsel. They knew this little boy, or so they said. They still marked him as the piano banger. The opinion that Luddy Newton was no angel would harden as it became evident over the years that one of his distinguishing traits would always be an irrepressible frankness. In time, he bowed to their assessment, and this accepting blame for their unease shaped to a large degree his formative years.

He never lost his first inclination to accept people as they were and to offer himself to them just as he was. Nevertheless, when his audacity had gone too far for others to be comfortable, a succeeding gravitation would suck him into a troubled isolation. There in the seclusion of self-inspection, he would call down condemnation on his head. But before he had a chance to grow morbid, he would draw on an inborn tranquility, and this sent him out once again wearing the same lack of guile and an extra dose of humility.

As he grew, he looked and listened a lot. He believed others knew more than he did, a rarity among pubescent boys, and this abnormality thrust him into voluntary, even eager, servanthood.

Taught in the Scriptures since he was a very young child, he longed to oblige God, but since he couldn't see God with his eyes or reach out and touch his hand, he felt he served God in enabling others. Setting little store by his own capacity, this was an easy thing to do, and he enjoyed it, and it gave him a happy spirit.

Most crises he met head-on, bounding back from a bruise with little evident damage. He considered each day a brand new gift and looked on each person he encountered in it as a friend; this had procured a happy childhood, and over the years evolved into adult composure. Almost never had the boy been outwardly flappable, and neither was he when grown. He had those bouts with unsureness and blame within himself, mostly short-lived, but occasionally to the point of asking why God should bother with him.

As he advanced to manhood, he became all the more frank, friendly and eager to help, but his utter openness stood him in a corner, and people thought even his willingness was odd. He knew them better than they knew him. In fact, in spite of his having grown up among them, they hardly knew him at all. Perhaps because it never occurred to him to push himself, people overlooked him; it was so unusual to encounter self-effacement that they forgot he was there. But he was not the inorganic nobody that some assumed him to be. Along with the maturing of mind and body, there waxed within him a sentient imagination and with it ideas, dreams, and goals. To him, however, they seemed to be prisoners deep within, unable to emerge either by themselves or with his help. A few times he had shared his thoughts with others; but only friends who for one reason or another had passed from his life—and in more recent times, Harry Churtle—had found them of any worth. This he accepted. Mostly in talking to him people smiled and changed the subject, whatever it might be. They smiled, but did not laugh outright, because they had to admit that Luddy Newton was, despite all, a good and well-intentioned person, one who undeniably possessed a loving spirit. They'd have felt guilty if they'd openly injured such a fellow Christian.

Luddy, indeed, had grown into an even-tempered, optimistic, cheerful fellow. But on the way there had been those hills and valleys in his life's marathon. The time, for example, that he mailed in three side panels from cereal boxes for a beginner's course in space exploration. Eagerly awaiting the mailman each day, he counted on this instruction to launch him on a career that, before he was twenty, would send him walking from Mars to Jupiter with the same ease by which he now covered the distance between his home and Jefferson Middle School. In a little over a month the packet arrived—a certificate of completion, an astral map showing the planets on each June 21, and a four-page leaflet reviewing John Glenn's orbit of the earth. Before the day ended, he sorrowfully decided his future was tied to earth's potentials. The next morning he awoke to the glorious thought that he might someday join the FBI.

Rather than becoming an astronaut or federal agent upon graduating from high school, he was glad to land a job as an attendant at a gas station. He enjoyed wiping crud off a windshield and grinning broadly at the face that suddenly appeared behind the sparkling glass. But with self-service coming in, this career posed a limited future. He jumped to stock replacement at a supermarket. The day he made this change was a happy one, the start on his new job coinciding with his first date with Karen Fitzgerald. No girl before her had let him court her. For three years they went together, and at age twenty Luddy was not quite sure of his intentions, but was not particularly bothered by his indecision. His older sister said drop her, his younger said to marry her. He let them talk.

They had a date coming up Friday night, a skating party at the local roller rink. He asked what time he should pick her up. Seven, Karen said. He might not get off work in time for seven. Seven, she said again. If not at seven, he needn't come around.

At 7:45 he phoned and said they didn't have to go to the party—they could just sit in the lawn glider in her backyard and swing and well, you know . . . there in the dark.

"You're not talking to Karen. This is her mother."

"Oh, hi, Mrs. Fitzgerald. You and Karen always did sound alike. It's fun talking to you, Mrs. Fitzgerald, and I'm sure we've got lots to say, but when we're finished, can I talk to Karen?"

"She's gone."

"To the roller rink—by herself?"

"Gone to get married."

"Married? Golly, we *can't* get married right now. I'm still in my dirty old work clothes."

"She went with Benny Foresman."

"Benny? Oh, go on, you're pullin' my leg. They'd need a license to get married."

"They've got one. He acted on faith, got it a week ago. Showed up here at five minutes past seven and told Karen what he had in mind. Now they've gone off to find a justice of the peace who will marry them."

"If that don't beat all! I'm surprised to hear it."

"Are you? For at least two years she's waited for you to pop the question. She gave you a deadline for tonight."

"I thought she meant skating. Since I had to work late I brought her home a nice geranium from the store. Oh, well, I guess it'll still be in bloom when they get back from their honeymoon." Shortly after that he moved into the YMCA and for the next two years spent a lot of time working out in the exercise room and swimming. Then he met Meribel Matson.

They got along fine. Neither was given to haste in their relationship.

For thirteen years they went to church together, every two weeks visited the public library, once in a while ate at Denny's or Big Boy before taking in a PG-rated movie, and while she lived, spent Thanksgiving with her widowed mother. Once a month they phoned his mother and father, who had retired to Florida. Often when she had a Saturday off from her job at Kmart she prepared lunch for him at her home. When finally the YMCA opened its ground-floor parlor to women visitors, she occasionally stopped in to read *The War Cry* or *Life* magazine, and if he were in, he'd come down from his room and listen as she read aloud the items she found particularly interesting.

He was thirty-five, she thirty-two. They were discreet in all things, never sat hunched together in church as some couples did, held hands in public only when he helped her down a steep flight of stairs or over a puddle in the street, said only things to each other that could someday be repeated by others without embarrassment. And he frequently shared with her the contents of a little plastic bag which he always kept handy in a pocket—jawbreakers, round candies that in size were somewhere between a golf ball and a marble, and almost as hard as either.

He thought she was the nicest girl, or woman, in all the church—even the town. She wasn't sure what her feelings were toward him. Pity, probably—for a start. She thought it terrible the way others slighted him. Maybe she loved him—a little. At least she had tried to imagine what life would be like married to him.

Pity or love, she nurtured their relationship, believing it good for them both. Now and then he wearied of the suffocation—some weeks he felt like not checking out any books so as to break the routine of returning on schedule to the library. At times he thought about marrying her, but on those rare occasions he hinted at it, she gave no indication of sharing his thought. At other times, it was she who touched on the notion of marrying him, but clearly then he was not in the mood and apologized that he was not.

The two were not so wrapped up in each other that romance or even friendship was the sole center of their worlds. For Luddy, interests ranged broadly, certainly among them the church and his job. For the last eight years he had driven a recycling collection truck for the county's Public Works Department.

And now there was fresh momentum to his life. He was the newest member of Rosewood Fellowship's Board of Deacons.

Chapter Two

Gilroy McAfee's custom was to ask for comment on an issue starting with the most senior—hence, the wisest—deacon and working down to the most neophyte, which, since last month's election, happened to be Luddy Newton. Voting, in which the chairman polled the deacons individually, was carried on in the same fashion. It made his meetings neat and orderly, every moment under full control.

A man given to habit, McAfee wanted to be charitable, as the Scriptures admonished. But conducting the Lord's work, whether one led the singing or a business meeting, was to him a ponderous responsibility. The burden of leadership branded him a crotchety old man. White hair laced with yellowed strands betrayed his age; a bending frame unmasked the cares that for too long had perched on his back. Yet, there remained strength and unflinching determination. Pink cheeks emerging from abundant sideburns, along with a still generous belt line, buttressed the notion that he might have been the original Santa Claus, but at some point he was dismissed for his perpetual scowl.

He himself was the senior deacon, now in his fourth term, with only the mandatory one-year hiatus interrupting his long tenure. Being senior, he spoke first on an issue, not as a divine right of his office, but as consistent with the logic that ruled him. After stoically delivering a well-reasoned viewpoint, encompassing both pro and con, he expected others to approach a subject with similarly detached assessment. So well-schooled were the deacons in his fairness doctrine that indecision crippled much of their deliberation. Sometimes they sat around a table in a classroom in the church basement for three hours saying little that hadn't already been said and at the end failing to wrap up a single piece of business. After one of the seven board members moved out of town, tie votes were common, when votes were taken, and matters at hand were tabled for another month.

One such item was a long-festering question—should the Sunday school hour be switched with the morning worship? Preach then teach, or teach then preach?

"A change would have good points and bad," McAfee said in a little speech that the veterans on the board had heard now for five months. "I have my feelings on the matter, but to be fair with you men I want to hear what you have to say. Pastor, let's start with you."

Technically, the Reverend Mr. Barrett was not a member of the board, but the chairman practiced professional courtesy by early on seeking his counsel.

"I could accept the switch," Peter Barrett said, speaking slowly after considerable reflection, a position already disclosed when, on previous occasions, the subject had been raised. "Yet, I do recognize the possibility of some pitfalls."

"You bet your life there'll be pitfalls," snapped Gordon Hayes, a man in his forties who usually spoke only when spoken to. "You're going to lose some housewives who'll cut your sermon to go home and start dinner."

Blurting out this unsolicited warning, he sent a shock through the little circle of men. None could remember such an outburst in a meeting conducted by Gilroy McAfee. What brought it on—from Gordon, of all people? Each old hand, including Gordon himself, looked around, seeking an explanation. Nothing differed in this meeting from those that had gone on month after month for years—except that tonight Luddy Newton was among them. Could Gordon's eruption have been ignited through some strange electricity radiating from their new member who as yet had only said "hello," but who, it had to be admitted, was quite unlike the other members of this body?

Whatever the cause, the jolt detached more tongues, each soon striving to outtalk the others.

"I just figured church always came first."

"First things first, I say."

"With Sunday school ahead of church, people who find it hard to get started on Sunday should be awake by worship time."

"There shouldn't be as many late-comers to church."

"We could move church to the afternoon."

"That's my nap time."

"You sleep in church now. So what would be different?"

"You can be sure the choir will take that hour to practice instead of going to class."

"You let 'em get to people first, Pastor, some of those teachers will steal your stuff."

Where were the dispassionate, carefully crafted arguments and their balancing rebuttals, discreetly offered only when asked for by the order-loving chairman? At this moment, pouring forth in a torrent, nothing but competing prophecies, each shouted in escalating volume for fear that one might drop unheard. Two or three stood to declare their views. Fingers were pointed and fists shaken. A preacher's cuss word fell neatly into a momentary pause. There had never been a deacons' meeting, at least under Gilroy McAfee's leadership, like this. *Something* was in the air.

Their comments captivated Luddy, who was content to sit on the sidelines. He had always held pastors, deacons, and choir directors in reverence, but now that he was one of them and was hearing opinions as if they were the prejudices of ordinary people, he saw these men in a new light. They were, after all, human. He scratched an itch on his back and in doing so threw a shoulder out of joint, something that happened commonly.

With a windmill rotation or two of his arm, and with a clearly heard clack of bones, he slipped his shoulder into place again quite as easily as it had slipped out. These maneuvers had abruptly halted the racket. All eyes focused on his convolutions. Those who had witnessed these windups before were always fearful that one day he'd generate enough thrust to send them all airborne. His arm, however, was back in place again. He grinned, an assuring grin that all was well once more, and with goodwill his only motive, passed around his plastic bag of jawbreakers. The calm he'd produced was not lost on the chairman.

Luddy wasn't necessarily the youngest man present. None, however, had a more innocent face. No line caused by worry marred it. Neither did guilt nor shyness nor suspicion dim the sparkle of his bright blue eyes. His mouth was perhaps a bit too wide for his face, but when he laughed he used it all completely and to great benefit. His expression was often a cross between a smiley face and that of a contented cow.

He laughed now—not a full laugh—but more than had been heard in meetings of the board. A teacher stealing the pastor's sermon points! He could see a black market set up in the vestibule.

"Evidently, you've got something to say, Fig, so say it," ventured Harry. He may not have realized that by issuing this invitation to speak he usurped the chairman's prerogative, or if he did realize it, tonight it didn't matter. Of all present, Harry probably was the only one who admitted friendship with Luddy. To Harry's mind, it was a one-sided friendship. Do unto others, you know... Like the Bible said somewhere, help the weak, lend your second cloak and don't expect to see it again. Luddy could do nothing for him, so Harry figured the guy was a good subject on which to practice being virtuous.

Because Luddy appreciated a friend, any friend, he didn't object to Harry calling him Fig, which others no doubt thought derogatory. But nobody would stick him with a nickname, Luddy reasoned, if he didn't like him. Wasn't it Harry who had nominated him as the least troublesome of three questionable options open to the electorate?

"You really want my opinion?"

"Speak up, Fig. That's why you're here."

"Well . . ." drawled Luddy, shifting a half-consumed jawbreaker in his mouth. "Well, I'd say you'll solve the problem about church and Sunday School if you figure out which came first, the chicken or the egg."

The explosive laughter was cut off by Gilroy McAfee's heavy breathing and his pink cheeks turning red.

"Hmmm," he said with grinding composure. "May I call to your attention, my friend, that we are here for the Lord's business, which—need I remind you?—has no call for levity."

By his reprimand, McAfee regained control of the meeting. He wanted no more of the debate that would have sullied the minutes had Bill Lennox, the clerk, been prone to record more than just the tally of votes, a secretarial style that necessarily kept the transcript brief. To protect the decorum, the chairman called for a vote and committed himself in starting the balloting.

"I myself think it wise to keep things as they are—Sunday school to follow the worship hour, as it always has been. But I don't mean to influence you."

On this singular night he didn't—not with three members who, when it came their turn, voted rather hyperactively to the contrary.

"As of now, we are tied," McAfee said, and there was gloom as well as fatigue in his voice. "Ludlow, it is your decision."

"Me? I've got to break the tie?" It was Luddy's first meeting, his first vote, and already the pattern of Sunday activity for a church full of people rested on his easily dislocated shoulder.

"Why, I—I—" He started to say "church first." It came out "Sunday school before church."

A slight rumble was all that was heard from the losing side because McAfee, as if turning over a page that was never again to be read, abandoned the old and, suddenly reinvigorated, brought forward a new matter.

"We are authorized by the budget to purchase Bibles for the pew racks."

He began consideration of the topic by saying he had always venerated the celestial language of the King James, and still did, but had to admit there were passages, especially the complex syntax of certain epistles, that left him somewhat confused. He clung to old-fashioned virtues, and always would, but at the same time prided himself on keeping up with the times. Having spoken his mind—clearly, he hoped—which version did the pastor favor?

"Well, as a matter of fact," Barrett said, "I dip into a half-dozen translations in preparing my sermons, but reading the Bible in publicthat's something else."

For the second time tonight, the deacons acted as Rosewood deacons had never acted. To a man, except for the oldest and newest members, they advanced their choices spontaneously, vigorously and with bias. The King James, the Revised Standard, the New International—and several other renditions of the Scriptures were presented, defined, attacked, and defended. Toward eleven o'clock the will of the house came down to two, the traditional and a modern. Before the chairman could call for voting, it was apparent where each deacon stood, except Luddy, who with malice toward none said he hadn't read a Bible yet he didn't like. Once more, his vote promised to be the tie-breaker. But there would be no vote. Rather than yield further to this newcomer, to place the clay of future activities in his molding fingers, Gilroy McAfee used his discretionary powers and postponed the decision—"until next month."

The end of the night's unwritten agenda neared. As usual, McAfee prepared to demonstrate his devotion to democratic rule by resorting to a monthly ritual. The time had come for each man to propose an idea that, if adopted, would better the household of faith. McAfee himself had nothing to alter present practices and, by his forbearance, obviously judged them just short of heaven's perfection. If anyone felt otherwise, they would at this time be heard.

The pastor said the chairman was right, of course, but he had one little request. Could they sing the Amen at the conclusion of the hymns? Somehow, an amen completed the textual thought, and singing this quieting coda would prevent Sadie Raye, the organist, from ending every song on a high-note crescendo, which resulted in a round of applause by some of the more emotional among the occupants of the pews, and occasionally, a standing ovation.

Gordon Hayes reported the women were complaining that the kitchen needed repainting.

"Are we to go through that again?" asked an apprehensive Harry Churtle. "They were six weeks settling on a color last time, and then four of the gals walked out while preparing the Every-Member Crusade dinner. Said the new pea-green walls gave them headaches."

"Careful who you call a gal," said Gordon. "My wife was one of them, and my health insurance never did cover all her prescriptions."

As McAfee's slightly crooked finger came around to point at them, others mentioned a broken window in the toddlers' nursery, the need to keep an eye on the teenagers in the back rows on Sunday evenings, and the peeling paint on the ball atop the steeple. The window would be fixed, the teens placed under surveillance, and the paint jobs, inside and out, scheduled.

"Ludlow," said the chairman in a fatherly tone, "I don't expect that you as the new man here can offer a constructive criticism tonight. Perhaps in the next month or two—"

"Sure I can," popped Luddy, surprising even himself. Probably the free-wheeling of the others had ignited a fuse within. "How about if everybody wore their name on their suit or dress on Sundays. That way, it'd be easy to put names and faces together."

"You mean name tags, Fig," asked Harry, "like you wear at a convention?"

"Well, I've never been to a convention. But when I drive the recycling truck, I wear a badge on my shirt that tells all my customers who I am."

"Yes, well, thank you, Ludlow." And by the expression of his appreciation, Gilroy McAfee buried the name tags—possibly for eternity.

"One more item, gentlemen," he continued. "As you know, because of the vacancy on our board, we postponed the election of your chairman. I am now ready for you to express your wishes."

For as long as any could remember, someone at this point had always proposed that their present and highly respected leader be persuaded to continue in office one more year. Tonight's meeting, however, had been different—men speaking out of turn and in no turn at all. In this strange environment, Harry Churtle was about to suggest the unthinkable—that perhaps they ought to consider making a change. He hoped to elevate Bill Lennox from clerk to chairman. But just as Harry opened his mouth, and before a sound could emerge, he was cut off by Luddy Newton. It was Luddy's first unsolicited offering of the night.

"You do a pretty fine job, Mr. McAfee, kinda loosey-goosey, like a hippie at the opera, letting everybody speak their mind and all. I'd be in no big rush to fire you." Despite the discomposure caused by the unconventional phrasing, his suggestion promptly won loud and unanimous backing.

It couldn't be denied that a peculiarity had governed tonight's meeting with an errant atmosphere abetting it and that the cause had to be laid to something. Both winners and losers of the one completed contest—over the Sunday school—knew instinctively the source of irregularity was Luddy. But before he laughed that time or made that facetious remark about the chicken and the egg or cast the deciding vote unaided by him they had already thrown over McAfee's time-honored rules and every man rushed to speak his mind just as if he were jawing at a pancake breakfast or the weekly luncheon of the Kiwanis. They hadn't done this before Luddy's election, nor even dared contemplate such sedition. Maybe it was Luddy's mere presence or his honesty or free spirit oozing onto them, a trait that people should have recognized before they voted him in.

Following adjournment, on their way out to the parking lot two of the losers on the Sunday School question accosted him.

"For an opener, you had quite a night. I hope you don't bust open with pride," one said.

"Me? Should I?" The thought puzzled Luddy.

"You decided the matter."

"I did? I only cast one vote, same as you."

"Just remember what St. Paul says about novices."

"In which version?" Luddy asked with a sly grin. He sensed that a quarrel was starting, and he did not like to quarrel.

"If they'd had drivers of recycling chariots in those days," the other losing partner conjectured, "Paul probably would've written a word or two about them, too, and their thinking they can take over and run the church."

"Oh, my job is scriptural, all right. Haven't you read where they picked up the scraps after the five thousand were fed?"

What had got into him for a quip like that? Had his presence on the deacon board affected him as it possibly had the others?

"It's a good thing we don't have bishops at Rosewood. Before you could be elected, Luddy, you'd have to marry that girlfriend of yours. First Timothy."

"Yeah. What's with you two? What's holdin' you back? For years, the whole church has wondered about that."

Chapter Three

Marcia phoned Luddy at the YMCA and said there was a job she wanted him to do.

"Sure," he said.

He'd been saying "sure" to his sister from the day his tiny lips first formed the sound and a year or two before he knew what the word meant. In fact, those knowing him best said the two words "yes" and "sure" played from an automatic disc lodged somewhere in his throat.

He felt no imposition. He hadn't the vaguest perception that he often stretched himself for the benefit of someone else.

"It was just something I wanted to do," he'd explain.

He took for granted that, being single and independent, he had no one but himself to please. That his pleasure sprang from the common virtues made it easy for him to please others as well. He did not like to disappoint anyone by turning them away. If he'd had a middle name, it might have been Willing.

In part, Luddy took after his father. Claude Newton had been crusty on the outside and banana custard within. He bequeathed only the pudding to his son, and because there was very little coating to encase it, people often took advantage of Luddy's soft and open heart. As a boy, he regularly washed the dishes because hot suds were hard on the hands of his sisters, and he dried them, too, when either Marcia or Leeann complained of a headache. He stepped back and allowed cuts in the school cafeteria line if, in melodrama, a kid threatened to faint from starvation. He volunteered to umpire or to keep an eye on the equipment if in choosing up sides one more selection would make the teams uneven for baseball.

But when committed, there emerged the bulldog spirit inherited from his mother. Falling darkness never stopped short his lawn mowing. One summer when the family was on vacation the car died on the highway; it was Luddy who walked five miles under a broiling sun to get a can of gas and walked back five miles, hustling all the way. He finished every book he started, always buckled his galoshes, endured pain in the dentist's chair, and outlasted his daring teenage buddies in every game of chicken.

In school, his fame excelled his popularity. "Let Luddy do it" became the drudge's badge. Because he trusted too many of his fellow students when they failed to merit his trust, he wound up being the goat.

One day a dozen senior class boys recruited Luddy to rebel against the rule that girls were not allowed to serve as president of the student council. In a secret meeting in a corner of the boys' locker room, each conspirator agreed to make a poster challenging the rule. The next day, in homeroom period, they would at precisely nine o'clock shoot them up over their heads, flabbergasting Mrs. Harris, their teacher, and starting a protest that would sweep through the school and throw out the antiquated rule.

In morning homeroom as he sat at his desk, his poster concealed on his lap beneath his desk top, Luddy looked around at his confederates. They smiled mischievously and nodded toward the clock on the wall. Two minutes to nine . . . one minute to nine . . . thirty seconds to go. The second hand swept to the hour. Up went Luddy's sign, and with it not the signs of the other boys, but a chorus of wild laughter.

"ELECT A GIRL. IMPROVE CENTRAL HIGH."

Luddy waved his sign, turned it for all to see—and realized that as a crusader he fought alone.

"Ludlow Newton!"

Mrs. Harris was impressed—but not in the way Luddy had hoped.

"You think you can use my classroom to propagandize your ideas? Radical ideas as they are, diametrically opposed to school rules, a particular rule that has been in effect as long as I have been teaching in this school?"

Some of her students, and their parents before them, supposed Mrs. Harris had come with the building, probably was left in a classroom by mistake when the plasterers and painters had completed their work and pulled out during the administration of Harry Truman.

"Well, Mr. Newton, I believe Mr. Wardell would like to see your placard. I strongly suggest that you take it down to his office—right now!"

It was just as the boys had planned. Who cared about electing a girl as school president? A laugh was what they had aimed for, and Luddy and his predicament had given it to them—a laugh promising to last all day—in the classrooms and chemistry lab, in the gym and locker room, in the cafeteria, and especially during study hall in the library.

But the girls cared. An hour later, Luddy emerged from the principal's office, bearing not his sign but the look of a whipped puppy. Two dozen girls mobbed him. Halted midway up the stairway opposite the office, three of the perpetrators of Luddy's embarrassment couldn't believe this display of hero worship. Their hoots of derision faded to low, mournful whistles. The very girls who wore their varsity sweaters were leading the cheers for this champion. How could the guy pass so quickly from being the butt of a prank to the sheik of a harem?

Thoroughly inflamed, the girls made Luddy their candidate for president. He won their vote, but lost the election. The boys controlled the counting of the ballots.

The day after Chuck Beeson was installed as the new council president, an announcement came over the public address system from the school office.

"Last night," the principal began, "the Board of Education adopted a new policy. Hereafter, girls will be permitted to run for student council president. They will have equal rights with boys under a new rule which the Board has named 'Newton's Law of Eligibility.'"

What was there about this fellow Luddy Newton that turned black into white and caused the sun to stand still?

But the job Marcia had asked him to perform would severely test the charm that seemed to envelop him.

"You know Beulah Simms—she's one of the sweet old widows in the church, a saint if there ever was one. Her sink is stopped up and rather than her paying thirty dollars an hour for a plumber, I said you'd drop by and unplug it for her."

"Sure, Sis. Tomorrow morning, first thing."

He was used to helping out widows and old maids. For one it was changing the oil of her car. For another, coaxing her cat out of a tree. Sometimes he washed walls and changed furnace filters and rewired the plug on a TV cord. He always refused pay, deeming sufficient compensation the thanks and plates of cookies and knitted mittens they showered on him. He phoned Mrs. Simms to tell her he would come—Saturday was his day off from driving the recycling collection truck. She informed him she'd be at her daughter's all day—Laura was bringing home her newest baby. But the kitchen door would be unlocked, just go in. The tools her late husband used—the plunger, and what did he call it, a plumber's serpent?—

she'd leave on the counter next to the sink.

It was a simple task to free up the sink drain. There was no need to use the snake. He wiped off the plunger and laid it on the counter. As he extracted a raspberry jawbreaker from his plastic bag, his eyes lit on a magazine next to the toaster. What was this, *Far-Out Follies?* Under it was another, *Peephole*. He thumbed through each. The explicit photos and the text he read here and there shocked him. These must be the kind of mags the jumpers on his recycling truck were always talking about. They would be classified, he had no doubt, as pornographic, though there was nothing in his experience to confirm that.

For more than half an hour he turned over page after page, gawked at the pictures in amazement and read things here and there that were neither in his vocabulary nor had ever before entered his mind. Then his curiosity satisfied, he carefully replaced them next to the toaster, ran water down Mrs. Simms' sink to test it, and left.

Saturday night was library night.

"I don't think I'll look for a book to check out tonight, Meribel," he said as they entered the building. "I want to look through the magazines instead."

While she lost herself in the stacks, he perused the periodicals rack, searching from *The American City* to *Yachting*. Not one of the library's offerings resembled those two magazines in Mrs. Simms' kitchen. If they couldn't make the grade at the library, what did that say about the widow's reading habits?

In the parking lot, he unlocked the door of his car. As Meribel was about to slide in, he puckered up his lips and came within an inch of her cheek. She suddenly turned and in panic shoved him away.

"Luddy Newton! What do you think you're doing?"

"Well," he said, apologetically as well as with disappointment, "I thought a little kiss wouldn't hurt anything."

"How dare you! Do you think you can kiss me without my permission?"

"Sorry." He was now fully penitent. "Guess I got carried away. Want a jawbreaker? I got a peppermint."

"No. What kind of magazines were you looking at in the library?"

"Not the library," he confessed. "A couple in Mrs. Simms' kitchen this morning."

"Mrs. Simms? That saint? What were they?"

"Girlie, I guess you'd call 'em. Right out on the counter, next to the toaster."

"How did they get there?"

"Who knows? They came from the adult bookstore."

"Did she tell you that?"

"She wasn't home. It was stamped on the covers."

On Sunday Meribel confided to her best friend that it was terrible you couldn't trust anyone today—imagine Mrs. Simms leading

Luddy down a crimson trail. Her friend casually mentioned it to her sister, and this good lady to a friend, and that friend to Bessie McAfee.

Wanting to be fair, one of his abiding traits, the chairman of the Rosewood Deacon Board looked up and down the sidewalk and across the street into the windows of the drugstore and detecting no recognizable person, swiftly entered Mac's Adult Bookstore to check out this hysterical nonsense that Beulah Simms, active in the Women's Missionary Society and an alto in the choir, had purchased pornographic material in this den of iniquity. He felt in need of a bath the second he stepped across the threshold. A couple of patrons interrupted their prurient scrutiny of the store's offerings long enough to make sure that he who entered was not a police officer brandishing a night stick. Gilroy McAfee hoped the place was not equipped with those cameras with which banks surveyed their lobbies, resulting in films that sometimes made it onto the six o'clock television news. Mustering more courage than he had used since confronting Rosewood's second-to-last minister to inform him he was fired, he stepped to a raised platform where a young man with long hair and Fu Manchu fingernails sat next to an old hand-cranked cash register.

"Yeah, Pops. Your taste in books, videos, mags, you name it—we got it all. Just look around and bring it to me along with your cash. No need to blush. I've seen it all."

"Well, that's not what I had in mind."

"What then, paraphernalia? Rubber goods?"

"Not that either."

"No? We are a specialized shop, you know. If it's *Black Beauty* you want, or the *Bobbsey Twins*—them we ain't got."

"Hmmm. Might I ask you a question?"

"From the looks of things, maybe I oughta be asking *you* the questions. I'd say you've been around a lot longer than me—and in an extra thirty or forty years or so a guy can learn a lot of stuff. If you get what I mean."

He laughed, his cackle riveting the attention of the store's customers. McAfee's pink cheeks darkened to red. The chairman of the deacons straightened his tie and pulled down his jacket in motions attributable to a man of dignity. If this steward of the devil's reading room mistook him for another perverted client, the fellow couldn't be too smart or very acute in his judgment of human character. A man of seventy-plus no doubt had learned a good many things in his long span of life, but to suggest that he, Gilroy McAfee, had lent either mind or body to fleshly subjects—it was enough to spin him on his heels and march him out the door.

He let his ire cool and with determination opened the business that had dragged him inside.

"You probably don't remember any particular customer," he stammered, "but a woman—"

"No problem. I remember every woman that comes in here. Partly because there ain't too many of 'em, but mostly because they're—women."

"An older woman. Say maybe sixty, sixty-five. Always wears a flowery hat. Possibly bought a couple of your magazines."

Lasciviousness turned up the corners of the youth's mouth.

"Remember? Sure thing. Three old gals maybe a week ago. They asked for the most risky thing we got."

"Risqué?"

"That, too. Risky because what they wanted I had to pull out from under the counter. We keep 'em there, you know, to hide 'em against when the cops send their plainclothes spies around, which I can tell you ain't. But yeah, they bought magazines. Scooped 'em up. One bought a couple issues, another just one, and the third, four, I think. I'll bet they had a great weekend!"

Painful as it was, Gilroy McAfee called a special meeting of the deacons for Thursday evening. Because two of the three elderly porno shoppers were members in good standing at Rosewood Fellowship they were asked to be present.

In front of the full board and the pastor, McAfee put the question to them as gently as he could phrase it. Yet, stripped of its soft-leather veneer, it asked, "Did you ladies buy pornographic magazines from Mac's Adult Bookstore?"

"Yes," came the forthright answer of Beulah Simms, and her companion nodded in agreement.

"Hmmm," said McAfee, introducing a stunning silence.

"Hmmm," he said again.

"Yes, we each bought magazines that the clerk brought from under the counter." Was she going too far? He hadn't asked about the degree of their transgression. He'd been willing to settle on generalities.

"That does square with the report, Mrs. Simms, that such literature was observed to occupy a spot on your kitchen counter."

Beulah Simms stared long and hard at Luddy Newton, her sink unplugger. After ample time to slay him with the daggers in her eyes, she turned back to the inquisitive chairman.

"Louise here and Rachel Givens, whom I doubt you know, and I—the three of us—bought the most salacious material we could readily find."

"You did?"

"Certainly we did. We now possess the ammunition to fire the first shot in our campaign to padlock every porno shop in this town."

"You're in a campaign to—"

"Yes. Pray tell, Brother McAfee, should there be any other reason for three old widows to enter Satan's realm and partake of his despicable feast?"

"Well, no, of course not."

The chairman sent Luddy a look matching that of the abused woman.

The cloud of suspicion hanging over Mrs. Simms and her fellow warriors did not completely dissipate until the sheriff, armed with a warrant based on the research of the three ladies, raided Mac's and thereafter instead of there being four targets for their closure campaign, only three remained.

Chapter Four

Luddy felt bad that he had wronged Beulah Simms. He himself hadn't reported her to the deacon board, and when Meribel had pulled from him about the magazines, he hadn't expected that bit of information to go any farther. And neither did it occur to Meribel, nor the person she told, nor those next in line that they were links in a chain of misconstrued intelligence. Luddy blamed only himself; it was his brash presumption toward a virtuous old lady that lay at bottom of this shameful injustice.

He apologized to Mrs. Simms, offered her the choice of a lemon or vanilla jawbreaker, but she waved him off too quickly for time to temper his guilt. A day later, hedged in by the faded brown walls of his tiny room at the YMCA, he tried looking back at the affair with some objectivity and concluded he would never amount to much; he was irresponsible, a natural-born troublemaker. He recalled a time when he and his little sister played with a ball in the living room and he knocked the portrait of an old family patriarch from the wall, breaking the glass and ripping the picture. Before his mother could come upon the damage he departed "just a few minutes early" for a meeting of his Boy Scout troop, leaving Leeann to face discovery and punishment alone. He now feared that with this second episode of reckless behavior in twenty-five years he was creating a pattern, and that depressed him as he seldom had been depressed.

For a week back then he had dried the supper dishes for his sister, and this voluntary chore quickly expunged his guilt and led him back to his natural state of equanimity. And now, a quarter of a century later, he foundered in a depth he'd never before known; if anything could lift his spirits from the pit in which his offense against Mrs. Simms had sunk them it would be his driving the recycling truck.

Being part of the County's recycling effort was very important to Luddy. Each morning when he pinned his name badge on his uniform it was as if he pinned on a day's ration of privilege. He was proud, and grateful as well, to be a member of the team that was saving the forests, saving the minerals, saving the animals, saving the whales, saving the oceans, saving the babies, saving just about everything that moved or didn't move, that breathed or remained ınanimate, that was targeted by the minds far superior to his own that made up the day's list of salvageables.

The week following the appearance of Mrs. Simms before the deacons, Luddy's daily tours of duty had thrust the most acute pain behind him. Early on this clear spring day there was no sign of rain, the temperature was unusually warm, the tulips were beginning to lend the world their color, and Luddy whistled as he drove his giant vehicle down Travis Street. His two jumpers were quite athletic this morning—it appeared the crew would make their rounds in record time. If they kept to the pace throughout, he stood a good chance of getting back to the garage in time to be one of the first in line to have his truck washed, and this would mean he then could go over it with a polishing cloth himself. Luddy liked a clean truck.

Rolling down the 900 block he heard a shrill voice call from behind the truck. In his mirror he saw a woman in bathrobe and babushka running toward him.

"Garbage man! Garbage man!"

Some drivers of recycling trucks would not have heeded the call, Luddy knew. They'd consider the term an insult to their profession. "Can't she see the garbage is still at the curb?" they'd say. "We take nothing but recyclables."

But Luddy was a man of broader understanding. Someone had a need, and quite evidently thought he could help. He stopped his truck, pulled on the hand brake, and jumped to the pavement. "Yes, ma'am."

The woman striving to catch the truck pulled up square in front of him, quite out of breath and clutching her robe.

"Oh, thanks for stopping," she said, panting heavily. Then after pausing to scrutinize his face, she added, "Do I know you? I think we've met somewhere."

"We have, Mrs. Simms." Luddy readily recognized her, though it was evident she was uncertain as to where their paths had crossed.

Possessing this advantage and having suffered much from their recent encounter, he might have suggested she was mistaken, or perhaps they had once bumped carts in the supermarket. But it did not occur to Luddy to dodge anticipated unpleasantry.

"Last week, remember? I did your sink, then we were both at the deacons' meeting."

"Oh, you're Mr. Newton. I see your name now on your badge. I guess I never did thank you for unstopping my sink drain."

"Yeah, well . . . when we met we had other things on our minds."

"You were the one who saw the magazines in my kitchen . . ."

"Yeah, I'm the one."

". . . and over which Brother McAfee jumped to such a ridiculous conclusion. How that usually sensible man could ever have thought that I . . . well, never mind *him*. I have a favor to ask of you, Mr. Newton."

"Oh, sure," he said. Perhaps she'd allow him to purge his guilt, after all.

"You took my newspapers."

"Yes. Newspapers are recyclable."

"I need them back."

"Back?"

Luddy's two jumpers seldom advanced more than a single house ahead of the truck, and now they slumped against it, glad for the respite. But hearing the plea for dumped papers, they rolled their eyes and groaned.

"We got a ton of newspapers, lady," one of them called to her.

"Well, really, I want only one paper, just one page of that."

The jumpers looked in the bin into which newsprint was tossed.

"I can see forty stacks in here that ain't been smashed together yet," said one of them. "Even so, they're all pretty much mixed up together."

"You want . . . your papers back?" stuttered Luddy. He shifted his purple grape jawbreaker from one cheek to the other.

"Just the one with the engagement announcement," explained Mrs. Simms. "You see, my friend's niece announced her engagement earlier this week, and I promised my friend I'd save the picture and article that appeared in the paper. Then I forgot and threw out the papers. Can you get it for me, Mr. Newton?"

Luddy nodded to his helpers. They hauled several bundles and armloads of loose newspapers out of the bin. They were stopped in front of 923 Travis. Here his crew began spreading out the papers.

"You say there's a picture of your friend's niece? So that would be a girl."

"A young woman. And her fiancé. It'll be on the society page."

"What name are we looking for?"

"Name? I don't remember. But she's blonde, and she wasn't wearing her glasses for the picture so she's squinting."

"And her boyfriend?"

"He looks like a jerk, because he is a jerk."

With the preciseness of a squinting blonde and a jerk as their target, Luddy, his two jumpers, and Mrs. Simms knelt on the somewhat damp lawn, unfolding papers, hovering over them, turning page by page, looking for likenesses of the betrothed.

"Beulah, what on earth are you doing down on your hands and knees?" demanded a voice a scant six inches from her ear. Looking up from her all-fours position and into the face of the blue-haired sixtyish neighbor bent over her, Mrs. Simms replied, "Oh, Rachel, just in time. Help us look for Jane Harrow's niece's picture, you know, the one in the paper the other night announcing her engagement."

"I guess I missed it," said Rachel, but her omission did not stop her from joining in the hunt. "Look for a blonde without her glasses and a jerk for a boyfriend," advised Luddy.

"Are you the boyfriend?" asked Rachel, who with difficulty dropped sacrificially to her knees, knowing full well she'd suffer arthritic pains for the next two days. In dutiful regard for her neighbor, she began turning pages and scanning them.

"He the boyfriend?" said Mrs. Simms. "Oh, heavens, no. Mr. Newton is a plumber, a good plumber—that is, when he's not recycling."

"Or," added Rachel, though hardly audible and arching her fuzzy white eyebrows, "when he's not reading other people's magazines."

Old Joseph Thornberry, the block's nonagenarian, chose this particular time to emerge from his house at 919 Travis for his daily walk around the block. With the aid of a cane, he lowered himself down his front steps and hobbled to the scene of journalistic scrutiny.

"Did my neighbor plant new grass?" he asked between wheezes as he poked a paper with his stick. "I understand they do spread papers around nowadays to keep the birds from eating the seeds."

Mrs. Simms, echoed by Rachel, explained their activity. His admiration for good-looking young blondes never having diminished, Mr. Thornberry joined the cause, though he had no choice but to stand and rifle the pages with the rubber tip of his cane. At that distance, each page was only a blur.

Luddy got up to turn off the truck's engine and returned to the search.

"It's gotta be here somewhere," one of his crew members said, though his voice was less confident than his words. "We just picked up her bundle back there four or five houses, so it had to be somewhere near the top."

The occupants of 923 were at work and unaware of the activity on their finely manicured lawn. The curious performance there attracted most of their neighbors, however, and a few more enlisted in the operation. After forty-five minutes ten searchers had gone through every paper recoverable from the bin in the truck, probably thirty newspapers each. None scored a success. Rachel excused herself; she remembered she'd left her teakettle on the stove to boil. Hurrying back to her house, which was one past Mrs. Simms', she halted abruptly at Beulah's driveway. There on top of a plastic barrel of wrapped garbage, a newspaper photo seemed to jump out and say, "Look at me!" She looked, craning her neck around to get a good look, then picked up the package and reshaped it to make the picture flat and clear.

"Here's your clipping, Beulah," she called excitedly, hastening with her prize back to 923. "It's here, wrapped around the garbage."

At that moment a sudden strong wind blew up from the east, wider than a dust-devil and only a little short of gale force.

It was brief and in the days when men wore hats it would have sent a few gentlemen scurrying in pursuit of their fedoras. So little to be wondered that the papers covering the lawn at 923 were its victims today. The swift clearance left depressions in the turf from heels and knees as the only visible evidence of the recent industry on that choice real estate. Documentation elsewhere, however, was abundant. Three hundred newspapers, perhaps three thousand sheets of newsprint, flying on the wings of a March-like gust in April, can light in almost as many places. These did, westward as far as the eye could see. Papers festooned trees and shrubs, littered porches, rested against steps, stuck on chimneys, draped over parked cars, lay inertly on lawns clear into the next block, waiting for another burst of wind to carry them even farther away.

"Oh, thank you, Mr. Newton," gushed Mrs. Simms, who believed in putting first things first. She probably failed to see the black and white blanket that covered a good portion of the neighborhood; her sight beamed on the man who had come to her rescue. "My friend Jane will be so happy to get another clipping."

"But it wasn't among the recycles . . ."

"If you hadn't stopped . . ."

Luddy's attention was not on Mrs. Simms nor the neat package of garbage she held to her breast. He was wondering how he was going to retrieve those newspapers.

"Man, you're in for it, now," exclaimed the senior of his two helpers. It was clear neither jumper claimed any responsibility.

Luddy was already halfway up the trunk of a tree to snatch a billowing paper from its branches.

"This neighborhood ain't been so tee-peed since the high school won the Thanksgiving Day game," laughed a volunteer among the neighbors. "You drive the truck slow-like, and we'll all pick up as we go along."

But not all picked up nor went along. Rachel had disappeared into her house, presumably to pry molten copper off her kitchen range. Old Mr. Thornbury was tap-tapping his way down the sidewalk, uncertain as to what had delayed his daily exercise. Mrs. Simms, shielding her precious packet of garbage in one arm, did what she could under the handicap. Two other neighbors joined her and the recyclers to make up the retrieval team. They had gone just past the corner and had started to tackle the next block when a van pulled alongside to the right of Luddy's truck.

"What in the name of ecology is going on here, Newton?" the van's driver, rolling down his window, yelled to Luddy.

"Oh, hi, Mr. Lacy. You out from the office?"

"No, I'm settin' in front of the TV at home with a beer in my hand."

"That's a joke?" Luddy's mouth turned up in a tentative grin. It could go all the way or he could pull it back into solemnity.

"I'm not out here to make you laugh, you idiot. Now what's goin' on?"

"Some papers blew away."

Luddy sighed. Looking straight through his windshield, he was afraid that under the circumstances any answer would be a redundancy.

"I'll say they blew away. Back at the office we got three calls from irate householders. Can't you keep your truck under control? You can be sure *this* will go down on your record."

"We weren't expecting the wind to blow like it did."

"And I wasn't expecting you to be so far behind schedule. Do you realize it's already nine-thirty, and you've hardly covered any of your route?"

"We had a very good start."

"I suppose you were malingering over coffee back there at Wendy's."

"He was doing no such thing, mister."

Mrs. Simms deposited an armful of gathered-up papers in the bin and strode between the truck and the van, stopping inches from Lacy's livid face.

"I heard what you said, sir." She spoke like an aroused citizen.

"This man here has been nothing if not the soul of kindness. Why, do you know what he did?"

"Never mind, Mrs. Simms," Luddy said, trying to cut her off. Compliments, especially before third parties, made him squirm.

"Why just last week he unplugged my sink for free, and today he stopped when I asked him to, and he and his helpers, along with some of my neighbors, found a newspaper I desperately wanted back from the truck since it carried a picture of my friend's niece and her jerk of a boyfriend."

"This the lady you unplugged the sink for, Newton?" asked Lacy, all of a sudden more curious than angry.

"Yeah, yeah." Luddy ducked his head. He revved his engine. "If we keep going, we can gather up the rest of those papers before they start blowing again."

"I heard all about you," the boss said to Mrs. Simms, and this time he was grinning, or perhaps more accurately, showing a bit of a snigger.

"Me? What did you hear about me?"

"You got any more of those magazines you want to recycle?"

Luddy's foot fell hard on the gas pedal, lurching the truck ahead, so far ahead, in fact, that he failed to hear the good lady's reply.

Chapter Five

Two consequences of Luddy's perusal of Beulah Simms' pornographic magazines lingered on. Meribel, not understanding how this poor man's curiosity could have enticed his nose into such salacious material, maintained a mild pout. And from time to time Mrs. Simms was newly embarrassed by a reference on the part of someone who did not know, or who chose not to acknowledge, that she dealt in the lascivious only for the purpose of running it out of town.

How his boss connected the Mrs. Simms of the recycling route to the woman whose magazines had proved so captivating mystified Luddy greatly. He parked his truck at the county garage two hours late, after the wash rack had shut down for the day, and since then had combed through his brain over and over. He was sure he hadn't breathed a word of his find, or even of his unplugging the sink, to Harold Lacy or anyone else, except Meribel, and she'd wormed the part about the magazines out of him. But his foreman knew—obvious when he referred to the plumbing and then mockingly asked Mrs. Simms about *those* magazines.

On his way home from work, Luddy again drove down Travis Street. Weighted with a heavy heart, he rang Mrs. Simms' doorbell. Once more he felt obliged to apologize. After the nice things she'd said about him to his boss he felt like a slimy slug among goldfish—she must be thinking he'd blabbed to the whole recycling crew about her taste in literature.

"Oh, Mr. Newton. What a *nice* surprise!" From the gush of her greeting, you'd think he'd unearthed a long-lost diamond necklace. "Do come in this instant."

"Well . . . I can say it right here on the porch. I . . . I want to apologize—again."

"Apologize?"

"Yeah. For what Mr. Lacy said to you . . . about the magazines."

"Well, that was him, not you. Just like the other night it was Brother McAfee who evidently took me for some kind of pervert."

"I mean about my causing him . . . well, I don't know how he heard that I fixed your sink or came across the magazines."

"Why, like everybody else, I guess. It was all on the six o'clock news a couple of nights ago. Didn't you see it?"

"No. I don't have TV in my room at the Y."

"It was all there. How they got it is beyond me, unless it was that newswoman who came out to interview me. I didn't tell her much . . . well, she asked so many questions I don't know what I did tell her."

"Then it wasn't me who—"

"Gracious, no. And now that you're here, you're just in time to share my supper. I threw in a couple of extra chicken thighs for no reason. I said, 'Beulah Simms, someday you're going to entertain angels unawares. Be prepared.' I guess that time has come. I'd show you the clipping I pasted on pretty rose-colored paper for my friend Jane Harrow, the one whose niece is getting married, though I can't say much for her choice in men—but I've already sealed the envelope."

"That's all right. It was in the paper around the garbage, not in the recycling stack."

"Yes, and only a small part of the picture was stained—his face, mostly. But without you, it never would have been found. I'm sorry about the citation for littering which that ugly-tempered policeman gave you. I heard he caught up with you on the next street over. Too bad. Well, come in. Throw your coat on a chair there and sit down at the table. I'll have another plate and the food on in a jiffy."

Later in the evening Luddy drove to the church with a full stomach and a light heart, rather, with a heart lighter than it had been when he rang Mrs. Simms' bell. Not all was right. There was Meribel. They'd gone together to the library Saturday night, as usual. But Meribel spoke rather pointedly when she asked what kind of magazines was he going to read while she looked for an uplifting biography.

"National Geographic," he had replied.

"The undressed pygmies, I suppose."

"Maybe I'll just check out a book. I don't have to have pictures, you know."

He hadn't tried to kiss her since the aborted attempt on that fateful evening. In their ride home and the next day to and from church she wouldn't laugh, only grunted a *huh* each time he told a "funny."

But his new friendship with Mrs. Simms having endured a most unusual day, he proceeded with spirits buoyed like a corked bottle in heavy seas. It was time for the monthly deacons' meeting, a regular session, the recent one over the Simms affair having been specially called. Tonight they would again take up which version of the Bible should be bought for the church pews.

Over the past month no deacon had changed his mind in regard to the King James versus a modern translation. Once more a tied predicament landed squarely on Luddy for a decision. He did not want to disappoint anyone, so in angling for an answer to please all finally said, when pressed for his vote, "Why don't we all learn Greek? Then we can go for the original."

That bit of erudition unnerved Gilroy McAfee. Fearing to further entrust this sacred matter to one so spiritually raw, he exercised the prerogative of the chair by withdrawing the question; there was no doubting that they needed more time to think and pray before making their choice.

Luddy would like to have known Greek, and Latin and Hebrew and Sanskrit. As well as astronomy, nuclear medicine, and a lot of other things. People often thought he was a dreamer, but he was not. He wasn't good at math and spelling, and if he had tried it, probably not at chemistry. But reasoning—that was his strength, provided you didn't rush him. He was rather slow in his thinking—not slow-witted—but he wanted to think things through and be certain.

It was the same in making friends. He liked everybody, and it was said he never met a stranger. But friends over acquaintances were few, probably because it took him a long time to think his way into a close relationship—whether with Meribel or fellow residents at the YMCA. He'd had a couple of buddies, but lost them. One, a classmate in junior high school, moved out of town. Another, a youth who lived across the street, was killed as he crashed his car into a tree on a curve. In that accident, Luddy was thrown from the passenger's seat into a ditch. By a miracle he survived with only a bloodied nose, a goose egg atop his head, and a dislocated shoulder. From that time on, the shoulder popped out of place periodically, but two or three full rotations set it right again. Months later he could laugh about his injury. "Some people are double-jointed in their fingers. With me, it's my shoulder."

Luddy had not been an attractive child. He was pudgy and of questionable proportions until well into his teens. His clothes were mostly hand-me-downs from various cousins, and because of his shape were poor fits. Not for the taunts of his peers, because he let them sail by unheeded, but to prepare himself, as he said, for the day he'd want a girl to look favorably on him, he cut back on his food intake and by huff and puff trimmed his weight. While not transformed into the All-American Boy, he passed credibly for a typical youth, if that designation was broad enough to include a ludicrous grin and an unruly cowlick that stood the hairs straight up on the crown of his head.

Passing into his thirties he surrendered some of his hard-won athleticism to the creep of middle age. But living at the YMCA, where he worked out in the exercise room, swam, and jogged on the roof-top track, he kept in reasonable shape, though he had to battle for time to care for his physical needs. When not driving the truck, there was Meribel to see; she might not want the heavy hand of romance, but she loathed feeling neglected. And there was his Sunday School class of boys to prepare for, to teach, to take on a hike in the woods and live the myth that they had to find their way out by a compass. His sisters often needed his help, either for themselves when their husbands traveled, or for a friend—unstopping Mrs. Simms' sink was no isolated chore of mercy. And now becoming a deacon promised to fill any vacant niche, not only with regular and special meetings, but with individual attention to the unnumbered tasks that needed doing in a congregation like that of Rosewood Fellowship Church.

Nothing weighty was settled at tonight's meeting. Discussion without intent of further decision filled the hours until eleven o'clock. Had the ladies decided on a color for the kitchen? Some had. Until all agreed, however, the job could not be started. What did the pastor think of Sunday school now coming before the worship service? Thankfully, no teacher had yet stolen his thunder, but perhaps this happy situation was due to the fact that the Reverend Mr. Barrett had launched a series of sermons from the Book of Ecclesiastes.

"Fig," said Harry Churtle, "do you notice an improvement in the behavior of your class of junior boys? Their breakfasts, after all, should still be in their stomachs."

"My boys are at the age when they have lots of energy, day or night, before or after meals—or at any time in between."

The following Sunday he and the whole church were to learn just how much energy twelve year olds possessed.

Luddy said it was his own fault. His lesson ran a little short. Who could expect boys their age to sit still until time caught up with them?

The class met in the basement in a ten-by-ten-foot cubicle formed by movable partitions of some five feet in height. The plywood panels rolled on casters, and at times when the basement became the church fellowship hall, they were pushed together and took over the storage space usually given to banquet tables. Deployed as they were each Sunday, the panels created four rows of classrooms. Fully adequate to keep wandering eyes within the confines, they did little to prevent the voices of fifteen or so teachers—and the commotion of children, especially the younger ones—from drifting over the tops of the panels and merging into one holy cacophony.

Luddy found it challenging to keep the minds of his boys trained on the lesson when next door in one direction a class of matrons spoke rather freely about the trials inherent in hardheaded husbands, and in the other direction a circle of teenage girls waxed keen on what is acceptable behavior for a Christian girl of, say, sixteen. But this the morning of the short lesson, his boys finally closed out the infiltration of outside voices. The allurement was within their room. Jamie Seacrist had brought a loaded water pistol and to his credit had kept it in his pocket all the while Luddy enumerated the benefits of twelve-year-old boys becoming modern Davids and Daniels. But with the "amen" of the teacher's closing prayer, out came the squirt gun. Immediately it became an object of admiration and desire.

"Lemme see it," pleaded each of the ten or so boys present.

"You can't shoot it," Jamie ruled.

"No, not in here," Luddy said in reinforcement.

The yellow plastic gun began its round-robin journey without incident, and because of the civility with which this treasure was handled, Luddy felt it safe to absent himself for a couple of minutes. He needed to surrender his teacher's lesson guide to the superintendent for passing on to a substitute. Next Sunday Luddy wouldn't be in church but would man the phones at the Recycling Center for the county's Earth Day observance.

All went well in the class until eventually the gun was passed to a boy rather large for his age, known by all, and feared by some as a bully. Will Rankin took aim on first one boy and then another, his finger tauntingly caressing the trigger.

"I said don't shoot," Jamie reminded him.

"And who's gonna make me not shoot?" sneered Will. He pumped the trigger, sending a jet streaming straight into Jamie's face.

Whether that was the water that broke the dam, releasing the pent-up lust of each boy to have his turn at shooting the gun, or it was the group ganging up on an already dubious member who broke the rule they had all abided by, bedlam broke loose.

Luddy returned at this moment.

"Boys! Boys! Sit down!" he ordered. But they did not sit down. Two fellows had wrestled Will to the floor, but he still held a tight grip on the water pistol. In spite of Luddy's efforts, three others joined the struggle, and in the scuffling Will shot a steady, copious stream that by some mysterious tracking cleared boys both on the floor and others who sat or stood around the battle zone and in a graceful arc looped over the top of the classroom divider into the midst of the senior women's class next door.

A lone shriek, a series of shrieks, a long, sad moan poured forth from the matrons' cubicle. "Bessie, what hit you?" a strong voice demanded of one who apparently had received youth's fountain full on her graying head and aging face.

"Water," Bessie McAfee answered. "Maybe the baptistery upstairs sprang a leak."

"Oh, Bessie, your beautiful hairdo—it's ruined."

"And your face. It's all streaking down your cheeks."

"That's what I get for being vain," lamented Bessie, and she gave way to tears. "God's getting back at me. Imagine, at my age spending all Saturday afternoon at the beauty shop just to be gussied up for our golden wedding after worship today."

Luddy heard the groans and weeping, but few of the boys in his class did. They continued to wrestle for the squirt gun, which now had spent its ammunition, the clothes of several of the boys proof of that fact.

"Now stop it, all of you," Luddy yelled, and behind him an assortment of Sunday School officers, teachers, matrons, and other pupils added commands of a similar nature.

Luddy pulled one boy from the writhing mass on the floor. He reached for another when his shoulder suddenly dislocated. Immediately going into his fail-safe remedy he clenched his fist and swung his arm like a windmill in a hurricane. He completed only one rotation. At some spot in the upward thrust his fist struck one of his pupils on the chin, spinning him off his chair and down on the now waning wrestling match. His victim lay inert and senseless—out cold.

In the rush to rescue the lad, perhaps the smallest boy in the class, a deacon or the Sunday school superintendent, or the pastor or possibly even Luddy himself, or one or more of his boys knocked over the panel that screened off the senior ladies, crashing it on top of at least three elderly women who had elected to stay put rather than to join the throng crowding the space next to theirs.

One of the three was Bessie McAfee. Knocked to the floor, she waited with some patience for rescuers to pull the panel from her. While a prisoner to this mayhem, she prayed a little prayer of thanks that though her situation was mortifying, her injuries seemingly were not life threatening; she also asked for a measure of charity which, despite her present feelings, she could at some time exhibit toward those who not only had compromised her dignity, but destroyed her dream of a perfect anniversary celebration.

She prayed, but the unspiritual feelings were not completely overcome.

Chapter Six

The special meeting of the Board of Deacons, called for a half-hour before start of the Wednesday night prayer meeting, got underway promptly at seven, timed by the ancient but trustworthy pocket watch of Gilroy McAfee. The only matter at hand in the mind of the chairman was what to do about Luddy Newton and his Sunday school class of incorrigible boys.

Before McAfee could clear his throat and by this muffled roll of thunder signal that the board was in session, Luddy started his small plastic bag of mixed-color jawbreakers around the circle of deacons. The first to receive it declined his generosity. A deacon not fully reconciled to Luddy's vote some weeks earlier that placed Sunday school before the starting time for morning worship, he handed the clear plastic pouch on to his neighbor with the caustic comment: "He's not going to bribe *me.*"

Luddy had passed around jawbreakers for so many years that the act had become more an instinct than a conscious handout, though undergirding it always was the donor's nature that held back nothing from anyone. To suggest that a bribe was making the rounds shocked Luddy, but the mere coupling of the word to himself made clear whom they would be discussing tonight. He hoped others wouldn't think he was trying to buy their favor.

"I've asked you to assemble for the purpose of dealing with a problem in our Sunday school," began McAfee. For him to forget an opening prayer, the problem had to be serious. It was. "It seems last Sunday we had a disturbance, the proportions of which cannot be overlooked."

The bag completed the circuit, lighter by only a single jawbreaker. Harry Churtle had extracted, as a debt to friendship, a sphere of licorice, but held it between thumb and forefinger, not sure what he should do with it. If the circulation of the candy was in some reverse fashion a hint of blackballing, the likeness was not lost on Luddy. He probably could count on only one deacon to support him.

His boys, not himself as their teacher, became the object to defend, and this he could do with conviction.

"They were just being boys," he said, jumping in, feeling the topic needed no further introduction. He rolled the half-finished wintergreen in his mouth to his other cheek. "Maybe more boys than boys ought to be in church, they were . . . well, just boys."

"You abandoned ship." Gilroy McAfee had shifted the target. He was as cold as an admiral at a maritime hearing. "You abandoned ship, and the pirates broke out in mutiny."

The charge was echoed by others. From the tone of the accusations, it was clear that this time Luddy's errancy was not going to be brushed aside. He would not be wrapped in Teflon. Ruining the celebration of a golden wedding was, after all, a fifty-year high among felonious deeds.

Luddy pleaded guilty to poor preparation that had left free time after conclusion of his lesson. He confessed to absenting himself for two minutes or so—abandoning ship, so to speak—and to failing to confiscate so non-Christian an object as a boy's water pistol.

"They're really good kids," he maintained. "It was my fault."

"This is not the first time they've got out of hand," rapped McAfee. Each accusation he disgorged with damning conviction. His habitual penchant for balancing a negative with a positive apparently had been routed by his wife's case against schoolboys and their mentors. "From her bed, to which her injuries sent her, Bessie told me the din that comes over the partition is disruptive each and every week."

Luddy could have echoed that statement, but always had considered commotion to be standard for Sunday School, so said nothing.

"Unless the members of this board decide otherwise, we must relieve you of your teaching duties."

"But that age was hard to control before Fig agreed to take the class," defended Harry Churtle.

"The decision is, of course, yours to make, you men of the board," cut in McAfee. "Unless I hear dissent, we will declare a vacancy in the junior department of our school."

Turning to Luddy, he said: "As you know, Ludlow, teachers are appointed, so teach at the discretion of this board. You were elected a deacon by the membership, so we have no power to remove you from this office."

Abruptly, he fell silent. Only to himself, Luddy finished the chairman's thought—*but we would if we could.*

Once more, Luddy sank to a depth of misery he had not to this point known. Why were these dark moods weighing in on him? Why the trouble with Beulah Simms, Meribel, his boss in the recycling program, and now with the whole church through his Sunday School class? These disturbances to his rooted tranquility had occurred only after his election as a deacon. He was not sure he liked this new world. Did some noxious inhalant come with the job?

His darkest remorse was not over disbarment as a teacher, but that the effect of his teaching had been so negligible that the boys seemed not to even notice his removal. He had looked on this class of boys as the one hope that his Christian witness meant something to someone. From the time he was a small boy himself he had longed to share God's loving redemption with people whose lives he touched, but somehow he always found himself distracted or speechless, and the door that was open suddenly slammed shut. With the boys, it was different. He had thought it was different. He believed he was making headway. But now he wasn't sure. Had his teaching merely gone in one ear and through impermeable ducts to the other? Had it all been in vain?

Bob Franklin succeeded him as teacher. He could take on the junior boys because, contrary to his expectations, he continued to bear a lesser responsibility in usher duties. Weldon Basker had refused to give up the center aisle, and Bob was forced to wait out another year for this plum. But as a teacher he lasted only three weeks. Then, in his turn, Weldon took over from Bob, determined to prove his greater aptitude. He gave up the class after two Sundays. Luddy grieved that as teachers came and went, so did the boys, but more went than came. Finally, Miss Thelma Moore was drafted to teach the four or five who remained. For fourteen years she had taught third grade in the public schools, so it could be assumed that with her appointment the problem was solved.

During these disheartening weeks, Luddy found balm in Meribel. Their relationship was improving practically day by day. It was not quite what it had been, but she no longer mentioned the word *magazine*, though if she'd been completely open she'd have confessed that particular periodicals, a couple of which she had not seen nor cared to see, came to mind when she was with Luddy and he clasped her hand or touched her arm. She thought it unfair that his class had been taken from him, and told him so as they dawdled over hamburgers one evening at McDonald's.

"The way Bessie McAfee carries on you'd think she'd been hit head-on by a Mack truck instead of a glancing blow by a sheet of plywood."

"I suppose it did bruise her," said Luddy, wanting to give the victim his sympathy.

"Bruised her pride. The woman's got enough of that to cover the two who went down under the panel with her. You haven't heard them complain."

"Maybe they complain but nobody ever hears them. Mrs. McAfee can get the ear of the deacon chairman every night just by pillow talk."

"Luddy Newton! Watch your language!"

Meribel bolted out of the booth and with determined gait marched her tray to the trash bin.

"What possesses you, Luddy?" she shot back to where he sat frozen in bewilderment, and half a dozen McDonald's patrons paused in their eating for an expected melodrama. "Your mind was never in the gutter before. It's time I was going home."

As they went out to his car with no word between them she half-mumbled to herself, "More of those magazines coming out."

Early the Monday evening after Miss Moore's debut as their teacher, two boys knocked on Luddy's door in the YMCA.

"Will Rankin! Paul Beasley!" Luddy exclaimed. "What a surprise!"

"Can we come in?" asked Will politely, and for this boisterous ox, obsequiously.

"Why sure," said Luddy. "I've only got one chair, but you can sit on the bed."

"Some of the guys wanted to come, too," began Will, "but I said me an' Paul'd come first."

If that's what Will said, that's what would be, thought Luddy. This hulk of a kid was fully capable of throwing his weight around with boys a good deal older than himself. Will appeared to be spokesman, not only for Paul and himself, but for those who were excluded from the visit. Perhaps he had bullied his way into this position, as he had bullied the boys in everything else from the first day of kindergarten. Or, possibly, the group had recognized that only a boy of his brass could do the job on which they were to send him.

"We're sorry you ain't our teacher anymore," Will continued. Sitting on the edge of the bed, he crossed his legs, recrossed them, and bounced his foot up and down, which bounced Paul who sat alongside him. Paul was one of the smaller boys, probably chosen as the brains to go along with Will's muscle. Will riveted his eyes on the colorful rag rug on which his stable foot rested. It was obvious that this mission, whatever it was, made him nervous, a state Luddy had not seen him in before.

"I shouldn't a shot off that water gun," he said without looking at Luddy, who had turned his desk chair around and sat on it facing the boys.

"I agree," said Luddy.

"I didn't mean to drench that woman's hair."

"I'm sure you didn't see her as a target, not over the barrier."

"And it wasn't me . . . it wasn't none of us . . . that pushed the divider over on the old ladies. It was that old man they call Mac somebody when he come rushin' in to see what was goin' on."

"Well, it's been some weeks since all that happened," said Luddy. "I'm sure most folks have forgotten it all by now."

"But we want you back as our teacher."

Luddy's world suddenly brightened. These were words he had given up ever hearing. Though he couldn't be their teacher, it was restorative to know that he was wanted.

"You've got Miss Moore now," he said, momentarily returning to reality.

"Yeah, but she can't do nothin' but talk. We ain't been out in the woods with a compass since they made you quit. And can you see Miss Moore—the guys call her Miss Less when she's not around—shootin' baskets?"

"Some boys have quit coming to Sunday school," said Paul, his first utterance. "Specially the ones their folks don't attend church so they don't have to come."

Will jumped up and crossed to the one window in Luddy's room. For a few seconds he peered intently through the glass, then said as if to someone he'd picked out on the sidewalk below, "I'm to blame. The guys said if I don't apologize, they'll kick me out." Turning to face the room, he added, "Not that they could do it if I didn't let 'em."

"Would it matter to you if the boys in the class weren't your friends?" asked Luddy.

"Yeah." Will faced Luddy squarely. "Yeah, it would."

For several minutes the three sat in the room talking—about reasons for attending church and Sunday School, about proper behavior in God's house, about forgiveness, about what made a friend, about a lot of things that had never been generated by the teacher's lesson guide. After a while Luddy said why didn't they go down to the gym and shoot some baskets. This they did.

Two days later five boys appeared at Luddy's door. Will and Paul had brought the owner of the ill-famed squirt gun and two others. Again they talked, with all sitting on the floor, and this was followed by basketball in the YMCA gym.

After three weeks of these frequent, willy-nilly sessions, Luddy decided that to get on with his own life and for the sake of the boys and their families some order had to rule. Being boys of eleven and twelve years of age, they naturally thought in terms of a club.

"Okay," said Luddy. "We'll be a club. But no substitute for Sunday school. I'll check each week with Miss Moore, and if you're absent from Sunday school without a good excuse, there'll be no club for you that week. Agreed?"

They all agreed, some with heart, some with sighs of capitulation. But stick with Luddy Newton and they'd have real fun again.

Fifteen or so boys trooped each Friday evening to Luddy's room; perhaps they horsed around so little because there was no space for roughhousing, just boys on the floor wall to wall, Will having chosen his spot first, the rest surrounding him. All week long Luddy had scoured the Bible for a verse or short passage that he deemed relevant to the lives of these kids, and on finding an appropriate one chewed on it with Meribel. Together, they'd striven for the practical angle for the evening's lesson. He felt he was not teaching, because sometimes the conversation went in directions completely surprising to him. Often they came to no closure, but that a few boys at least were stimulated to think about God's view of their lives became evident when without prompting they picked up on the earlier week's topic before allowing Luddy to shift them into a new path.

By eight o'clock they had quit the room for the gym or the swimming pool or sometimes—new experiences for most—the squash courts or wrestling mat.

Spring had come briefly once, then disappeared. Now the days were brightening again. Luddy felt the relief ushered in by warmer temperatures and golden sunshine. Enjoying this new season, he longed also for a change in the climate of his standing with Meribel. For while they were together almost as frequently as ever and talked freely about the boys and church and books they checked out from the library, there was something stiff and unresolved when, after everything else was said, they had only themselves to consider. Perhaps, he thought, the boys could help. While Meribel had kept in the background with no direct contact, she'd made all kinds of suggestions for activities and bull sessions and solving of problems which Luddy put into practice. They had talked about getting the club involved in some useful project. Why not, he thought, a project to benefit Meribel? It certainly couldn't hurt his situation.

Meribel lived in a small house near the edge of town. It had been her mother's, and Meribel shared it until her mother died. An ordinary bungalow on a rather large lot, it was an attractive place, with old trees and numerous flower patches. For several years Luddy had spaded the gardens, first for Meribel's mother and then for Meribel, digging carefully around the peonies and phlox and sunbursts and other perennials, preparing the soil for the large number of annuals that gave the yard its color all summer long. That was it! The club would rake up the old leaves, dig out the weeds and spent plants of last year, and turn the earth for the new assortment of flowers that Meribel would soon assemble. Instead of the succession of Saturdays required when Luddy worked it himself, a dozen or more nimble and energetic youths could do it all in one day, and the garden would benefit from an early start. And the boys would get good training in ecology, a subject important to Luddy.

They just showed up at six one chilly Saturday morning, dressed for winter, not the spring day anticipated, shovels and rakes and hedge clippers in hand, whatever tools the boys were able to round up at home.

"Work quietly," Luddy said in a hushed tone. They were gathered as if huddling before the Big Game. "I want to surprise the lady who lives here."

"She's your girlfriend, ain't she?" asked an impish lad, who then for cover slipped behind Will.

"No . . . well, yes . . . not that. She's a very good friend of mine."

"Will she help us do the job?" asked another.

"Maybe give us hot chocolate and cookies?"

"She sleeps late on Saturday, her day off," Luddy explained. "By the time she comes out of the house, we'll have half the work done. I can't wait to see the look on her face. Now, come with me. I'll show each of you where to work and what to do."

A great deal of young masculine industry was generated before eight o'clock, and to hasten progress Luddy staked out a plot for his own concentrated labor. The sun appeared through the thinly leafed trees; as it rose higher, jackets came off and the digging and raking and chopping began to flag. Trips to the water jug increased. Blisters on small hands were compared. Boastful calls were hurled from one end of the yard to the other. The project's secrecy was at an end.

Meribel appeared on the back stoop, robed in a housecoat, with her hair wrapped in a towel.

"Luddy, is that you?" she called. Throwing down his shovel where he had been spading in front of a rose bed, he hurried toward her.

"What's going on here?"

"Surprise!" he called. The work stopped. The boys drifted toward the back door. "Your garden will be ready for your new plants in a couple of hours."

"You mean you and the club are spading?"

"And raking and trimming and weeding and everything else that needs doing," he said, with a grin resembling a crescent moon.

"But can't we expect another frost or two?"

"In that case, I'll spread newspapers over the new plants you put out," Luddy promised. In the best of spirits, he laughed, "I'm good at that—spreading newspapers around."

"I must have really slept. How long have you been here? I took my shower and went out to the kitchen for breakfast, and for the first time saw people in the yard."

She stepped off the small porch and walked to one of the garden plots.

"Where are the peonies?" she asked. "Who dug up this garden?"

"I did," Will answered with some pride.

"But my peonies, they were coming fine. What did you do with them?"

"I didn't see nothin' but weeds and old, dead plants. I dug 'em out like Mr. Newton said."

"And the sunbursts!" She ran to another spot in the yard, and the entourage followed. "They're always there, even under the snow, and now they're gone! And who cut back my lilacs? All the branches about to bear blossoms are lying there in that pile under the bush."

She began to cry. Luddy offered his handkerchief and tried to lead her back to the house and away from the carnage his crew had so energetically produced. But she pushed away and ran into the kitchen, slamming the door behind her.

"We've made some terrible mistakes," Luddy said, as much to himself as to the club members. "I should have supervised more instead of digging myself."

"Can we go home now?" one of the boys asked. "I'm gettin' cold an' I gotta go."

"I'm tired," complained another. "I feel like crawlin' back in bed."

"Yes, you can go," Luddy said, exhaling heavily.

The boys quickly dispersed. He himself went up the three steps to the back door and turned the knob. The door was locked. He sat down on the steps, his head dropping to his knees.

Chapter Seven

Rosewood Fellowship Church wore a geographic name—the rose from Rosedale Avenue, which ran in front of the building, and the wood from Woodmere Drive, alongside it. It was so named by the Reverend Ernest Thayer, founding pastor, who had named all the churches he started after their adjacent streets.

Pastor Thayer believed the local church should identify with its neighborhood. Gilead, Mount Zion, and the names of the apostles were popular choices, he acknowledged, but a man or woman of the world might be less comfortable entering a church with a churchy name than going into one possessing an everyday familiarity. Rosewood had almost been Woodale, but the strong-minded teetotalers read into that name an insidious innuendo.

Rosewood identified with the subdivision in which it was located. Not always in the manner Pastor Thayer had envisioned, for the good Mr. Thayer was an exceptionally spiritual man. But physically, it was intimately known by everyone in the neighborhood.

"Continue down Rosedale Avenue," a householder would say in

giving directions to a friend on a first visit. "You'll come to the church with the white ball on top of the steeple; turn right on Woodmere—we're one block up the street."

Today, however, the white ball of Rosewood Church's steeple was no longer a meritorious guidepost. It was, in fact, becoming a neighborhood eyesore. The ball atop the spire badly needed a coat of paint.

The outside of the church proper and the square tower on which the steeple stood were in fairly good shape, having been painted some five or six years before. Climbing up the ever-narrowing shingled spire to reach the ball presented a serious problem. For this reason, this apex adornment had been neglected, probably for all the forty years it had been up there.

Talk was common around the church that painting the steeple ball would, however, be a picnic compared to putting a new coat on the kitchen. White was the only choice for the ball. Six colors and four shades of each had been advocated by a corresponding number of women, all of them strong-minded and every woman possessing impeccable aesthetic judgment. Climbing the steeple would be a formidable task, agreement on kitchen pigment nigh impossible.

Luddy—the deacon in him evidently pushing him to more aggressive enterprise—volunteered to paint the ball. But people were not so sure he should. What was he after, notoriety, acclaim for his bravery? Since the cancellation of the McAfee golden-wedding celebration set for the afternoon of the infamous Sunday school riot, Luddy had lost favor with member after member, not so much because his pedagogical talent was questioned, but because his little ruffians had deprived them of the year's social highlight. And now that the switch between church and Sunday school had had time to settle into routine, some longed for the old system, just as the Hebrews once longed for the garlic and leeks of Egypt, and, like Moses, Luddy was blamed for their dissatisfaction.

One who kept herself from this criticism was Beulah Simms.

"You're talking about Mr. Newton? Oh, he's the greatest! Thoughtful, generous, puts himself out. If anyone can paint the steeple, he can."

A few of her friends began to wonder if Beulah had become infatuated with a younger man, one, in fact, young enough that she might be his mother. To shield her from unstable feelings, whose nature she failed to perceive, they strongly hinted that Luddy and Meribel were quite established in their relationship, but Beulah saw neither their reasoning nor why it should be voiced to her.

"He fixed my sink. He found my newspaper. If it weren't for him, those wicked men running that bookstore would still be peddling their filth."

"But Beulah, it was Gilroy McAfee who pursued that case. And you yourself—"

"Gilroy McAfee can't hold a candle to Mr. Newton. Let's see that old duffer climb up that peak to paint the ball."

And because neither Gilroy McAfee nor anyone else stepped forward to risk limb and life, Luddy's offer was accepted.

After placing himself on line for this unwelcome toil, Luddy began wondering how he was to accomplish it. He calculated the base of the spire to be twenty-five feet off the ground, and the spire itself another fifteen or twenty, to the ball. Sometimes looking at it from a block away he doubted that anyone's neck need be risked for so inconsequential a protuberance as a knob the size of a beachball. Then, on his way either in or out of the church, he would crane his neck upward, and the flaking, rusting finial would fairly shout down at him: "Do it tomorrow!"

The question: How to get a rope up there. He needed a solidly anchored rope by which he could climb or be lifted from the top of the tower to the ball. He might try to lasso the spire and, clinging to the rope, inch his way up in the manner of mountain climbers, or do like those fellows he'd seen in the YMCA gym who, hand over hand, climbed ropes to the ceiling just because they were there. Or they could build a scaffold—all for slapping a bit of paint on a sphere the size of a beachball? Or maybe they could hire one of those industrial helicopters. He'd recently read in the paper that they came at a thousand dollars an hour. They'd need, what, maybe ten minutes? But the catch was, you paid portal to portal, so to speak, and the nearest for-hire chopper had to come from the East Coast.

That night, after futilely trying all day to solve the problem, Luddy dreamed he was at the base of the ball, and fortunately, his brain stayed in the gear of reality just enough to make him look around and see what held him to his perch. A long thick rope had been wound once around the spire and each end was held by a man on the ground—specifically Weldon Basker and Bob Franklin. Luddy's belt was connected to the big rope by a smaller line, maybe a foot in length, so even if a foot slipped as he clung to the rope, he would be held firmly in place.

Awakening, he picked up on the idea in his dream. Yes, he assured himself, it would work. Standing on the slim parapet of the tower, he'd call out to the men below to slacken their line a little. He then would lift the rope a foot or so, the men would draw it taut, binding it against the spire, and grasping the rope, he'd pull himself up a step. This would be repeated, step by step up the tapering cone until he reached the top. Almost like shinnying up a tree. Once there, he'd lift off the lid of his paint can, another attachment to his belt, extract a brush from his hip pocket, and slap the ball with paint. Oh, first, he might have to scrape off the rust and what remained of the old paint, so in the morning he'd write a note to himself to be sure and carry a scraper and wire brush.

He broached his plan to Weldon, and gaining his acceptance, to Bob. Each, however, learned the identity of his fellow rope holder, and two resignations were quickly submitted. But Luddy refused to let either back out.

"You were the rope holders in my dream," he said first to one then the other. "Since this plan is right out of my dream, I don't dare risk changing a thing. Besides, you're ushers, and in a way you'll be ushering me up to my seat at the top. Just pretend it's a seat up front."

He was more convincing when he reminded them they would be on opposite sides of the church and thus out of each other's sight.

The Saturday morning came for the "Scaling of Mount Pisgah," as Pastor Barrett had christened the venture, likening Luddy's ascent to the climb that put Moses in full view of the Promised Land. A large crowd had gathered, made up of both parishioners and sub-division dwellers, and as a particular contingent bent on cheering their hero, the boys in the club at the Y. In a pre-climb prayer for Luddy, Peter Barrett asked that he be given an experience more akin to Moses' view of the landscape than that of Balak, that renegade who used his lofty perch to call down curses on the Israelites.

"May he look down from his height and see us as Thou seest us."

That was going too far for some within hearing. Was Luddy Newton expected to come down from on high and issue his own commandments?

The slats had been removed from a sound vent for the bell in the upper reaches of the church tower, and through this opening Luddy emerged. A scattering of applause was engulfed by the wild shouts of nearly a score of boys, some whose voices puberty had changed and some who still squealed in high pitch. Hanging on to the frame of the opening until he could reach out a hand and grasp the rope, in place around the base of the spire as he'd planned, he stealthily inched along the tower's ledge until he was able to fasten his lifeline to the long, thick hawser. More boyish cheers greeted this achievement.

"Ready on the right?" Luddy called down to Weldon Basker. Weldon freed a hand momentarily, waved, and clenched the rope tightly again.

"Ready on the left?" Luddy yelled to Bob Franklin. Bob nodded his head, and those around him called, "Ready!"

"Let's go, then," Luddy cried. "Slacken, boys!"

His paint bucket joggled at his belt as he slowly, step by step, worked his way skyward, methodically carrying out his scheme. Painstakingly, he would lift the loosened rope, then give a yell for the ushers to take up the slack, and holding on dearly take another step. Slacken, lift, tighten, step. He walked all the way to the ball.

Luddy carefully held on with one hand and sent the other to a rear pocket of his pants. He felt his paint brush, but he was not ready to paint. Just as he had foreseen, the ball needed scraping—and he had no scraper. He had forgotten to write himself that note in the morning, and because there was no note, he forgot to load up with scraper and wire brush when preparing to ascend.

On the ground, Harry Churtle sensed Luddy's need. He ran into the church and soon came out with scraper and brush.

"Catch!" he called up to Luddy. He threw first the scraper then the brush, but neither attained the height of the tower ledge. Pastor Barrett took a turn. His pitch of the brush was wild, succeeding only in breaking a pane in a window of the sanctuary. Will Rankin, the biggest of Luddy's boys, said he'd try. He came the closest yet. Luddy might have caught the scraper, but in his effort to nab it threw his shoulder out of joint and the missile sailed on and struck him in the head, drawing blood, which quickly became a rivulet coursing down his face by way of an eye and into a corner of his mouth. Bouncing away, the scraper fell to the other side, and in spite of the instant pain from the disordering of his joint and the cut in his scalp, Luddy thought of the old game they as children used to play, Anty-I-Over. From up here, you certainly got a different perspective on the game.

Putting first things first, Luddy inaugurated his windmill rotation, and only after his bones snapped back into place did he extract a handkerchief from a pocket and apply it to his wound.

"I'm coming down," he called to those holding the ropes.

Everyone assumed the escalation to Pisgah was over and the peeling ball would continue to blight the neighborhood. The intent of Luddy's descent, however, was not to doctor his head and accept a disability discharge from duty. He came down only to firmly pocket the scraper and brush. Again, he started his climb. Having taken two steps upward, he heard the call of a familiar voice, but never before had it sounded in such panic.

"Luddy Newton! What are you doing up there?"

Meribel Matson had overslept on this Saturday morning, her day off, and knowing Luddy was meaning to climb the steeple, she rushed without breakfast to the church, believing her presence was necessary to his safety. He had described to her his plan for climbing, but it sounded academic, and the inherent daring did not register in her mind. Arriving now as he was once more airborne, the danger was spread out before her.

"Luddy, you'll kill yourself!" She bit heavily on a crushed handkerchief. She was sure he would die.

He waved without looking down. Would she really care? There had been pity in her call to him. But, did he also detect a hint of love?

"He's been up before," Gilroy McAfee said to Meribel. "He'll do all right."

Luddy once again clambered his way to the ball. This time he scraped off the rust and loose paint, patted the cut on his head with his handkerchief, opened his can of paint, sailed the lid into the trees below, pulled the brush from his pocket, spread the essence of new life on the naked, drab ball. As he worked, a couple of drops of blood plopped into the can. He reckoned the resulting pink to be so light that in peering at the ball from the ground only he would know its true color.

He worked carefully, making sure to splatter no paint on the black shingles that covered the spire. He searched the ball's surface to see if he had missed any spot. He had not. He was finished. Satisfied with his work, he twice pumped his fist in the air and gave a Churchillian "V" to the folk below. They responded with a roar, in a single loud voice forgiving him for costing them a golden afternoon in the church basement. The thrills of this morning outside had more than made up for that loss. Then with the job done and only the descent remaining, Luddy remembered what in his enthusiasm to do a job that needed doing he had forgotten—he was afraid of heights.

He wrapped both arms around the thin tip of the shingled spire. He looked upward, not chancing a look toward the earth that was far, far too distant below him. That old saying came to him, about something being as exciting as watching paint dry. Well, he didn't need the excitement, but the way he felt now he'd be clinging to this toothpick until the paint not only dried but began to peel again.

Down below, the boys of the club kept up their cheering for their leader, yelling his attributes directly into the ear of anchorman Weldon Basker. Nothing could he do about it as long as he stood there, pulling as tightly as he could on the rope, knowing that a man's life hung on his dependability. But with the job now done, he wondered why the order did not come to slacken, for Luddy to let himself down, step by step in reverse of how he had climbed to the top. He looked up at the figure high above him, expecting to catch some sign. The sun, moving ever higher, blotted out Luddy, the rejuvenated ball, and the entire steeple. Its effect on Weldon was the effect its brilliance had on most people.

"Here, hold this," he said in desperation to Will Rankin, and stiffened his upper lip. Will continued to shout encouragement to Luddy, with most of this big fellow's bellowing going straight into Weldon's ear.

"Grab . . . huh-a-huh . . . hold," Weldon ordered, "and hang on. I've got . . . to . . . to . . ."

He sneezed, in the process bending almost to the ground, and somewhere in the transfer of Luddy's life-guaranteeing line the rope escaped all hands and darted like a snake across the church lawn. At the top of his world, Luddy, at the precise moment of transfer, determined to conquer his fear, so relaxed his hold on the steeple and trusted himself to the rope. He thought it slack, and felt it becoming more slack, but that was his last thought about ropes and plans to dismount him. He fell head over heels, somersaulting backward as if hurtling down a mountain slope. All in a split second his fall and intermittent visions of the glistening ball comingled, the sphere against the sky shrinking from a beachball to a tennis ball and as the distance between them grew possibly would have deflated further but for the paint from his bucket that poured over him, closing his eyes and filling his ears and driving the taste of old blood out of his mouth.

Shock stupified the crowd below.

"Grab the rope!" someone coming to his senses shouted.

There was no need to grab the rope. It had ceased its mad journey across the grass, lying still at the base of the tower. Following it upward, the fearful spectators raised their faces to confront a man hanging off the tower, suspended by a slender nylon cord linking the now taut rope to Luddy's belt. He appeared to be doing a backbend in mid-air. Not only were both arms performing the windmill trick, but his legs pumped in bicycle fashion as well.

By some quirk—or was it the interceding hand of God?—the big, undisciplined rope had somehow become wedged on the tower, ending its free flight and saving Luddy from a plunge, probably headfirst, to the ground. By the dictates of no less a commander than Gilroy McAfee, Bob Franklin, on the leeward of this terrible excitement, slowly stepped toward the church and by his gradual easing lowered Luddy safely to the ground.

Meribel tested the strength—and sharpness—of her elbows to break through the crowd. She was the first to bend over Luddy as others stretched him out on the grass.

"Luddy! Luddy! Tell me, are you hurt?"

He started to turn on his right side, but grimaced. With less effort he turned on his left and spat out a mouthful of paint.

"Just my arm, where I guess I hit it on the tower coming down. And my knee. I think I have a lump from banging it someplace. But one of my problems was sure solved." Here he grinned, resembling every bit a white-faced clown. "I was wondering how I'd ever get down."

Meribel wiped paint from his eyes and face with her handkerchief, and for the first time seeing blood ooze from the cut on his head called for other hankies before falling next to her man in a faint.

Water from the kitchen brought her around, and paper towels from the lavatories did a fair job of cleaning the excess paint from Luddy and his clothing.

"Now, can somebody take their towels and clean up that mess?" he asked, pointing to the steeple. Generous white streaks and numerous little sub-streaks ran from the top to the bottom of the spire, sparkling in the sunshine against the blackness of the shingles.

"Not today," Harry Churtle said. And they wouldn't tomorrow or next week or for any time in the foreseeable future. Directions given to visitors to the subdivision would for some time to come instruct, "Come as far as the church with the streaked steeple and turn right."

By noon the crowd had dispersed, except for Luddy, a few of his boys, and the pastor. Even Meribel had left. She went home to fry zucchini and bake peanut butter cookies, Luddy's favorites. Their gala lunch would celebrate his successful painting of the ball, though that success was tempered in everyone's mind by the unintentional expansion of the original job. If she'd been the type to be more open to her friends, particularly her special friend, she might have said this super lunch would also be her way of saying her pout against Luddy was ended.

Weldon Basker and Bob Franklin were among the first to leave the scene, though, of course, not together. People had accosted Weldon for his negligence.

"Why'd ya leave go of the rope?" He was asked time after time.

"I thought that kid had it. I had to sneeze."

"Why can't you sneeze like everybody else. A sneeze is a sneeze and it's over. But, no, you have to go into contortions every time, doubling over and making such a production."

"At least," said Bob, "he didn't drop his teeth. Remember when the old set flew out and shattered against the steps of the church?"

Possibly because there were only two rope holders and he was one of them, Bob Franklin shared in the blame for Luddy's accident. Or it might have been that the members thought of these two ushers together. So as the panic eased and the postmortems began and the two saw they were to be the morning's goats, they quickly faded away, preferring to be tried in absentia.

Luddy stayed around for the purpose, as he said, of watching the paint dry. More truthfully, he ached in several places, not only his arm—not the one with the errant shoulder—and his banged knee, but also his middle, which at the end of his fall had borne the terrible tug of his belt. Followed by the more faithful of his club boys, he entered the church basement to wash up. When he saw the pastor carrying chairs from a storage closet to the sanctuary upstairs, he asked if he could help.

"If your boys would lend a hand, I wouldn't object," Barrett said. "You remember, the Methodist choir is joining ours tomorrow for a mini-concert in the morning service. I thought I'd get a head start in setting up the platform."

Luddy hobbled to the closet, which contained not only chairs, but at least two dozen limp, gold-sprayed balloons.

"Intended for the McAfees' golden wedding," the pastor explained. "But stuck in here and when the festivities were called off, forgotten, I suppose."

One of the boys took time out to blow up a half-dozen balloons. He tied a couple to his wrists and went back to the chair detail. That was the last Luddy saw of the balloons—until after Sunday School the following day and well into the worship service, after the combined choirs had sung and the pastor was in the middle of nailing down his three sermon points on the wages of sin, striving to make sure that the Methodists understood. One golden balloon, then a second, each filled with the breath of a twelve-year-old boy, floated gently downward over the heads of the rapt congregation, which soon became a ruptured congregation, and chose their landing sites among two hundred and fifty half-amused, half-perturbed churchgoers, visiting Methodists among them.

Possibly only one woman in all the congregation wore a hat, and it was on the pin that held it to her head that one of the balloons lit, and the blast of its disintegration served as a serendipitous exclamation mark to Brother Barrett's second point.

Chapter Eight

The night desk clerk of the YMCA trudged two flights up to the residence floor and after waking an exhausted bulldozer operator from a sound sleep and interrupting a grudge chess match needlessly, he finally located the door of Luddy Newton's room and gave it a sharp rap.

"Hey, you!" he shouted, and no one on the floor was quite sure whom he addressed. "Phone call for you downstairs."

Luddy opened his door, appearing in plaid pajamas, his right arm in a cast.

"For me?"

"For your grandmother, if you've got her hidden under the bed."

Reaching for robe and slippers, Luddy asked, "Do you know who's calling this time of night?"

"Some dame." Sauntering back down the hall to the stairwell, the messenger turned and leered at Luddy, who was following. "I doubt she's got a name—a real name. They don't, the kind that call guys in the middle of the night."

Luddy looked at his watch. Ten minutes past midnight. He had taken a sedative prescribed by the doctor and gone to bed early, hoping sleep would soon numb his three centers of pain—his broken arm, his banged-up knee, and the bruised muscles around his waist.

"Hello," he said, gently letting himself down onto the tiny seat in the phone booth.

"Luddy, this is Marcia."

"Hi, Sis."

"You sound sleepy. I thought I should call before you went to bed."

"Yeah, well . . ."

"Do me a little favor, will you, Luddy?"

"Sure, Sis. What is it?"

"David's going to a convention in Hawaii, so I decided the kids and I are going with him. Every family's allowed one vacation of a lifetime, so this might as well be it."

"That's great, Sis. Thanks for calling me up and telling me."

"I would have called you earlier, but we just got home from the movies, and a little last-minute shopping at the all-night Kmart."

"How long will you be gone?"

"Two weeks. Time enough for you to stretch out and enjoy yourself."

"Stretch out and enjoy myself? You're the one going to Hawaii."

"I mean in the house here. Did I ask you yet to house-sit while we're gone?"

"No, but..."

"You're a dear. Always so accommodating."

"When do you leave?"

"Tomorrow morning. Our flight's at eight-fourteen. You will take us to the airport, won't you? And come get us in two weeks? That way, we won't have to leave the car in the paid lot."

"About this house-sitting—"

"Oh, just the usual. The lawn may have to be mowed a couple of times. Dave meant to do it this evening, but we all needed to unwind before the big day so he never got around to it. And if you sleep in Robbie's room you'll probably want to replace the storm window with a screen. And while you've got the ladder out, you might as well change all the windows. I know we're into July, but we've got those heavy, old-fashioned kind of storms and screens, and we've just had no time to get it done. And don't forget to feed the dog a couple of times a day."

"Marcia, I've got a broken arm."

"A broken arm? From that paint job at the church? Oh, you poor boy. But how many hands do you need to feed the dog?"

"I was thinking more of the storm windows and mowing the lawn. But, no problem..."

In their good-byes at the airport Marcia promised to bring back a gift for her brother.

"A pineapple, maybe?"

"We'll see."

Luddy discovered that one man knocking about in a big house—with only a schnauzer, a hamster, and three goldfish to share the space—was not at all bad. Entertaining here was preferred to the Y. There, he and Meribel sat reading their library books or playing Scrabble or watching Jeopardy, always under the satyric eye of the night desk clerk. Here, they had the choice of a sheltered patio in back, a conventional living room, and a family room whose condition from wear and tear overstated the number of family members it really served.

Luddy shared his first evening as master of the estate with Meribel on an exclusive basis after he shut Hamburg, the schnauzer, in the basement and the dog's growls toward the strange lady were reduced to pathetic moans behind the stairway door. While the sun sank beyond the neighbor's ridgepole, the couple grilled hotdogs on the patio. Then hoping to find the house a bit cooler or, at the least, a haven from the rising tide of mosquitoes, they retreated to the kitchen.

"We should be able to find something here for dessert," Meribel said, opening the refrigerator. "A pie! Is that a lemon pie?"

"Lemon meringue."

"Did you bake it, Luddy? One of your hidden talents?"

"Me? Oh, no. Mrs. Simms did."

"Mrs . . . Simms? When . . . how . . . did she know you were staying here?"

"Marcia told her. Before she told me, I guess."

Meribel closed the fridge door.

"What about the pie?" Luddy asked, wondering why she did not bring it out.

"I'm allergic to lemon pie."

"Oh, well, I saw some chocolate-chip cookies in one of the cupboards."

"Here's popcorn. We'll finish off with popcorn. I'll make a caramel sauce. Now, you go in the living room and turn on some lights while I fix it."

He went as directed. In switching on a table lamp he noticed for the first time a piece of paper on the end table. It was a note left by Marcia.

> *I'd appreciate your doing these few things while you're here, Luddy. No particular order, and there's two whole weeks to finish them.*

The list contained eight items.

> *1. Pull weeds. Dave says ragweeds draw mosquitoes, so if you're bothered by them, you'd best pull out anything looking like a weed. They're particularly heavy all around the edges of the yard. We didn't get around to planting our usual garden this year.*

That was a new one on Luddy. He'd never heard that ragweed and mosquitoes held anything in common. But he lived in a tiny room at the YMCA, and Dave was a landowner, so Dave should know. Luddy determined to go after the ragweed first thing following work tomorrow. He glanced through the list, lighting on No. 7.

7. Never close Hamburg in the basement. He does things it takes a long time to clean up. Not worth the hassle.

He went on to No. 8.

8. When you have spare time, please, pretty please, clean out the fireplace. I'm ashamed to say the ashes are from winter before last.

That job shouldn't take long, he said to himself. But, hey, there was wood in a coal scuttle and a pile of newspapers next to the sofa—and wasn't that a book of matches on the mantle? Why not one more cozy fire? Using the materials at hand, he built up a blaze that confronted Meribel when she brought a huge porcelain bowl of popcorn in from the kitchen.

"Are you crazy, Luddy? A fire on a hot night like this?"

"I thought we could sit on the sofa here and guess the images the other person sees in the shape of the flames."

"Well . . ."

They sat on the sofa, eyeing the crackling sparks that leaped free of their source. The hum of the fire, the shifting of burnt logs and Hamburg's incessant moaning were the only sounds. As each dipped into the bowl of popcorn, their fingers sometimes touched and tentatively entwined. Meribel did not draw away, though she pulled Luddy back when he started up to turn out one of the unnecessary lights in the room. The popcorn was warm, the night air hot, and the waves from the fireplace were hotter still, yet they seemed not to mind. Whether it was all this heat or something else that mysteriously passed between them, their differences of the past months appeared to vaporize. "I've dreamed of sitting here like this with you," Luddy said, and prodding fate one step beyond, wished his lips might just for a second touch hers. He was realistic enough to recognize the impossible, however, so instead picked up Marcia's list from the end table. Breathing a sigh of contentment—after all, they'd never had a night like this—he vowed he'd finish every job on the list before the first week was out.

They had thrown on the last piece of wood in the scuttle. Perhaps there was more in the garage or basement, but he did not want to get up to find out—especially to go to the basement for fear of learning that Hamburg's reputation for careless behavior was true. So they sat, speaking little, and merely watched the flames diminish.

"You're so original to think of a fire in July," Meribel finally said, and her eyes reflected the soft glow of the dying embers. "But, Luddy, look. It's beginning to smoke. Shouldn't you do something?"

It was smoking. Flames spurted here and there, died back, and from their throes more smoke billowed into the room than circled up the chimney. For several minutes Luddy tried a number of fixes, but this insubordinate child of his creation would not yield. The flue was at fault. Cleaning the fireplace would also mean cleaning out the chimney. Overhead, a smoke alarm sounded, pushing Hamburg's decibels to a higher register.

Coming up from behind where he knelt, Meribel shouted in his ear: "Here! Take this!"

She held the popcorn bowl, which no longer contained popcorn, but water. It suddenly became too heavy, and she dropped it. Hitting Luddy's shoulder, it bounced into the grate and smashed into small pieces. The water doused both Luddy and the smoldering chunks of wood, sending up a column of steam in place of the smoke.

Fortunately, the shoulder did not belong to the broken arm, but was the one that could be put back into place by the windmill motion. Luddy performed this ritual, sitting on the hearth, soaked from the neck down. Meribel sat down beside him, and they both laughed.

After that, there was nothing to do but for Luddy to change clothes and take Meribel home. But he made her promise, and she was very willing, to return for supper again tomorrow.

"I'll do the cooking," she promised.

After the pot roast, she served up Mrs. Simm's lemon meringue pie.

"But, Meribel, if you're allergic to it, we don't have to—"

"Maybe a teensy bite won't hurt," she said, and stuck her fork in his piece. Tasting it, she jumped up, kicking over her chair, and choked into her napkin. Picking up the two dessert plates, she rushed them out to the kitchen.

"What's the matter?" Luddy asked, at first immobilized by her extraordinary action, then trailing her across the dining room. He swung open the door to the kitchen to see her slide the pie off the plates and into a trash pail under the sink, following this up by tossing in the rest of the pie, plate and all.

"It's rancid."

"It's what?"

"Rancid. Spoiled. Good thing you didn't eat any. I had a cousin once who ate rancid lemon pie, and he was laid up for a week. Terrible cramps."

Luddy dipped his good arm into the trash.

"Mrs. Simms might want her pie plate back."

"She might. But let's hope she scours it well."

The next day Luddy no sooner had gotten home from driving the recylcing truck when Mrs. Simms dropped by to retrieve her dish.

"Did you like the pie?" she asked as she picked up the plate from the kitchen counter.

"You bake a beautiful lemon pie," Luddy said. He hoped their conversation would not delve deeply into the particulars.

"I hope it wasn't too sweet. I may have put the sugar in twice. Did it taste too sweet?"

"I didn't taste it," Luddy said. That was a true statement. He had to be honest. "I mean I didn't taste the pie. We . . . threw it out."

"My pie? In the garbage?" She sank into a chair.

"It was rancid. Spoiled."

"Rancid . . . rancid. It was rancid. You said 'we.' You and . "

"Meribel. She took one bite and said it was rancid."

On the mention of Meribel, Mrs. Simms emerged from her shock and recovered to defend her reputation.

"That's funny. I've been baking lemon meringue pies for fifty-one years—fifty-two if you count the first one I helped my mother with. And not one, not a single one, ever before was rancid."

"Maybe it was that double portion of sugar?"

"No, I'd say Meribel doesn't like certain pies."

"Lemon meringue pies."

"As I said, certain pies. Mine."

Forward looking as she was, Mrs. Simms chose not to dwell on the ill-fate of past offerings. She took from her bag a garment unrecognizeable to Luddy.

"For your back," she said, handing it to him.

"What is it?"

"A girdle. It belonged to my late husband. He found it very helpful every time his lumbago flared up. You wear it around all day and before you know it your middle will feel as good as the rest of your body."

Luddy involuntarily flexed his bruised knee, tapped the cast encasing his forearm, and rubbed his cheek on the shoulder victimized by an errant popcorn bowl. With such reference points he had little hope for the efficacy of a girdle.

"Thank you, Mrs. Simms. You're very thoughtful. I'll wear it."

On their drive to the library Saturday night, Meribel asked Luddy why he sat so straight and stiff. He told her about the late Mr. Simms' girdle.

"You wearing a girdle?" she laughed. "I thought corsets and such went out with the bustle."

If either Meribel or Beulah Simms was even slightly jealous of the other, Luddy failed to notice. Both were fine women, the only ones in all his life who could come close in character to his mother. In Mrs. Simms he saw his mother's penchant for virtue, in Meribel her resolve to implant it around her. Mrs. Simms had one other trait that affected Luddy. She was helpless to pick up on the things her late husband had always done for her.

"Please come over and sort through all these papers the bank keeps sending me and help me balance my checkbook," she had said before departing the day she lent Luddy the girdle. He did and recommended she close out the account and start over at another bank.

"Phillip always replaced the furnace filters in July, but I haven't the faintest notion how he did it."

"Those tent caterpillars have lodged in one of my trees. I'm sure you know how to get rid of them."

Meribel complained that whenever she phoned him at Marcia's house he was never there.

"You're house-sitting," she said one day, "but whose house?"

The club met at Marcia's on Friday night. The family room offered plenty of space for their discussion, but, of course, there was no gym or swimming pool or racquetball courts. So, harking back to his childhood, Luddy taught them kick-the-can, which they played in the street. The boys thought it a great game. The neighbors hoped they would stop long before they were willing. They played on after dark, finding it fun to hide the dented soup can in the long shadows cast by the street light—until Will Rankin got mad and threw the can at the light, and whether lucky shot or skillful, broke the globe and plunged the whole block into darkness.

Dave, Marcia, and the children returned from Hawaii sunburned, cross from the long flight, and very much aggrieved that the hamster had died. Luddy contritely promised the children a replacement, but, of course, no other rodent on earth could take the place of the unfortunate Cheeks. Luddy was glad to retreat to his old room at the YMCA.

Ten days later Marcia paged him to the phone booth in the parlor to say she was sending over the gift they'd brought him from Hawaii.

"I should have given it to you sooner, but we just now unpacked the box we sent our extra baggage in," she explained.

His nephew Robbie brought it, a large flat parcel.

"Funny shape for a pineapple," Luddy joked.

"Yeah," half-grinned Robbie, for whom at sixteen humor possessed a different tint than it did for grown-ups. "Got to go, now, Uncle Lud."

"It'll just take a minute to unwrap it," Luddy protested. "Your mother told me you kids picked it out."

"I really got to head out. I'm late now for basketball."

He was in the stairwell before Luddy could tear the first layer of paper away. It was well wrapped, Luddy observed. Must be something of great value.

Finally, the gift stood naked before him—a velveteen picture of the surf before Diamond Head.

The Y had rules against nails in the wall. So Luddy propped the picture, not quite as large as da Vinci's *Last Supper*, on the dresser, but it blocked out the mirror. He tried it on the window sill, but the room went dark. The picture, which did have a nice gold-sprayed frame, ended up on the floor between his bed and the wall.

The next Friday night a couple of the boys hauled it out and the whole bunch oohed and aahed over it, proclaiming it a masterpiece of greater beauty than any that hung in the halls of their school. Luddy cut the discussion short this night. At seven, they'd start the club's swimming meet in the Y's pool. It was important that the event move right along, because the Y's own meet, involving fifty-some young members, was scheduled for eight o'clock.

The judges were in place, the starter had his whistle, the contestants were poised—all except Will. His trunks, always a bit snug on his generously endowed loins, split. The meet waited until alternate trunks could be found, not an easy task when the adult supply window was closed for the evening.

But start they did, and the competition moved along at a reasonable pace, but three races remained as the little hand of the wall clock rested on eight and the big hand snapped straight up to twelve. Officials of the authorized meet gathered in small, agitated groups, shaking their stopwatches almost as vigorously as they shook their heads.

Ordinarily, they would have ended the usurpers' monopoly of the facilities. But Luddy had persuaded the district's congressman to head the team of judges for his club's contest.

Twelve hours later, the last chore the night desk clerk did before going off duty to spend Saturday as he wished was to nearly break in Luddy's door in summoning him to the general secretary's office.

"Newton, as a resident here at the Y," this no-nonsense director-general began, "you are entitled to invite a reasonable number of appropriate guests to visit you in your quarters and to use our recreational facilities. But I've had reports that on Friday nights you actually bring in a dozen, fifteen, twenty boys every week, crowd them in your room for bull sessions that are not my business, and then fan them out for two or three hours in the gym, the pool, and every other facility we boast of possessing."

"You got it about right, there," Luddy said, nodding in agreement. "Some would like to use the sauna, but we've only got one kid who can stand to lose the weight."

"Do you realize that these boys in your club or your group or whatever you call it are costing us memberships for which, without your personal sponsorship of their visits here, we would be collecting much-needed dues?"

"Say, I never thought of that," Luddy said. "But, of course, a lot of my boys would qualify for junior scholarships."

"Last night I came back to the building a few minutes before eight, expecting to view our annual summer swim meet. But at eight-thirty you and your boys hadn't yet cleared the pool. I did not want to embarrass the congressman, so we waited until you finished."

"Well, thank you very much. I think he appreciated that we asked him to be a judge. People don't often call on him for the nice jobs. He said he hadn't enjoyed himself so much since he voted to raise congressional salaries."

"Well, you're finished now," the secretary growled. "No more private club inside these walls."

The core of the club was his former Sunday school class at Rosewood Fellowship Church. His connection to the boys there had been halted because of their roisterous behavior. Now they were put out of the YMCA. Where could they go?

He decided to approach the Reverend Peter Barrett and ask if they could meet in the church basement on Friday nights, not as the Sunday school class, which Miss Moore still taught, but more as a Christian Boy Scout troop.

"Usually, the church is dark Friday nights," Luddy said, presenting his case.

"It is," the pastor agreed. "And I have no personal objections, but you'll have to see Brother McAfee. He is, as you well know, the chairman of our deacons; he has a feel for what is right for the church."

Did Daniel fight to get into the lion's den? Did Joseph happily flee the humdrum of home for the fleshpots of Egypt? It was no more unlikely for Luddy to seek an audience with Gilroy McAfee.

To his surprise, he found the man more approachable than

expected, though, of course, a degree of austerity enveloped him. McAfee was dressed as if it were Sunday morning, and Luddy had never seen him dressed otherwise. On his part, Luddy was neat enough in a freshly pressed recycling uniform, though he felt a tuxedo would have been more appropriate. He had plastered down his ever-present cowlick, but now for this crucial one-on-one meeting a fistful of hair stood defiantly straight up on the crown of his head. He hoped that didn't make him look defiant to the chairman.

"So you've come to talk about your club of boys," McAfee said, assigning their conversation a category. They sat in the pastor's office, a small room off the front of the sanctuary. While Peter Barrett was out making his parish calls, McAfee often occupied his desk and swivel chair. In this setting he conducted interviews such as the one today with Luddy Newton, who was seated in a plain wooden chair. It lacked only a spotlight overhead as a replica of the third-degree seats that were supposed to be standard equipment in every police station. "They *are* the boys, are they not, who pushed the divider panel over onto my wife?"

"I heard it actually was someone else," Luddy replied.

"And who was that?"

"I'd rather not say, since it might be embarrassing."

"You're not saying I did it, are you?" The chairman fairly growled as he sat upright in his chair.

"I didn't say it. And by the way, how is Mrs. McAfee?" He really wanted to know.

"Her hurts linger on." McAfee sniffled, bit his lower lip, and once more leaned back, staring blankly at the ceiling. "She seems all right one day, then she'll have a sudden relapse."

Luddy's inquiry had turned the tide. He had strayed onto an obviously tender topic.

"Does she suffer in the back or around the middle?" Luddy thought he might lend her the girdle of the late Mr. Simms.

"I don't know. In the head, I'd say. Comes and goes."

Again he snapped the swivel vertical and bent toward Luddy.

"Life in my house over the past six months has been—" He looked around and softened his voice for what he wanted to say. "It's been . . . well . . . unpleasant."

He straightened up, wiped his lips as if to purge the word that might have escaped through them.

"Well, maybe more like the last six years," he added. "Or maybe sixteen. One evening her sister phoned to say she was arriving the next day for a visit. Bessie had a sudden attack. I worked until two in the morning, cleaning the house and getting it in order. All Bessie could do was lie on the couch and give me instructions."

They talked on, surprisingly with a good deal of amity and wandering outside the designated category—about the second pornography shop in town to close its doors, about the modest growth in Sunday School attendance since going to the new hour, about Luddy's parents and how much they had meant to the church, about McAfee's boyhood poverty during the Great Depression.

Without further buildup, Luddy bluntly asked, "May our boys' club move into the church Friday nights?" It was as if he had sprung a trap.

"Hmmmm," the chairman waffled, sensing a toe, at the least, to be caught in the noose. "Well . . . you've no doubt considered the positive points of such action. Have you considered the negative?"

"Yes. The negative is that if we don't have a place to meet my boys will drop out and drift away."

"But if you met in the church, Mrs. McAfee, taking into account her recent ordeal, would only get upset. She'd say . . . she'd . . . but . . . but . . . Oh, for goodness sakes, Ludlow, of course, you can!"

"We can? Thanks, Mr. McAfee. Thanks very much."

"Friday nights only. And if, *if,* the older ladies should, which I'm sure they won't, decide to put on a function on a Friday night, you are to take your boys on a hike at least twenty miles away from the church."

"That we'll be glad to do," said Luddy.

"And if that happens, I just might go with you."

The chairman slapped his thigh to set in cement the most decisive action he had taken in a quarter of a century.

Chapter Nine

Luddy drove his recycling rig down Travis Street. It was the regular morning for that part of his route, and on the 900 block he half-expected to see Beulah Simms at the curb, along with her yellow container of cans, bottles, No. 2 plasticware, and newspapers. He should have more than half-expected her; she had been there each time he worked the segment this summer, and she was there again this morning.

"You men deserve a cold drink," Mrs. Simms called as Luddy stopped the truck in front of her house, and his two jumpers emptied her bin and that of her neighbor.

They paused in their relentless scavenge for reusable materials destined to extend the nation's natural resources to at least the next generation. Ice-cold Cokes were indeed welcome in the July heat. Not many householders looked out for garbagemen or recycling crews. But Mrs. Simms was a good woman, Luddy often told his helpers. People like her made life pleasant.

He felt fortunate to have known in his time a lot of good people. There were his parents and yes, his sisters, and the Reverend Ernest Thayer, founding pastor of Rosewood Church. Luddy was too young to have known him well, but was not entirely unfamiliar with him by legend. He recalled a scene here and there that cast him as a jolly friend of children.

Today, of course, he'd put Meribel at the top of the list, and Harry Churtle and Bill Lennox, the church clerk, and Gordon Hayes who was another deacon, and someone he supposed he must not neglect when it came to naming good people—Gilroy McAfee. And Mrs. Simms, though his thinking in these terms had started with her.

He once looked on Gilroy McAfee as a difficult man. He didn't dislike him, because Luddy couldn't think of a single soul he really didn't like. But after their long talk together in the pastor's office—Pastor Barrett was another name to add to the list—after they'd discussed Mrs. McAfee's problem and covered a wide range of other subjects and even before the chairman gave his consent for the club to use the church basement, Luddy decided McAfee was a good man who'd been through wearisome times. Yes, definitely, Gilroy McAfee should be on his list.

What about Weldon Basker? Momentarily his gaze dropped from the curbs of Travis Street to the cast that shielded his broken arm. If Weldon hadn't let go . . . you couldn't really fault the man for sneezing. Occasionally Luddy sneezed at inopportune times, though he nor anyone he knew made a spectacle of it as Weldon always did. Weldon was all right, and so was Bob Franklin, his partner in keeping Luddy alive on the church steeple.

Jake and Carlos, his jumpers, were friendly fellows, quick operators, a little lewd in their speech for Luddy's tastes, but nevertheless faithful to their job, always putting in an honest day's work. Come to think of it, Luddy guessed he didn't know anybody who couldn't make his list of good folk. Oh, he was fully aware that the human race was cursed with a sinful nature and in need of redemption, but in this world so full of trouble and sorrow he believed he was of all men most favored.

He whistled as he drove the last block of Travis and cut over to Holcomb for the reverse direction. Joy flooded his soul. Over the past months he'd watched his joy rise and fall, and at times had come near losing it. But he was on top today. For one thing, he and Meribel were closer than ever in their relationship. And there were others he now held dearer. Having done most of the work in exchanging Marcia's storm windows for screens, Harry Churtle proved himself a true friend. Luddy's boss had not only decided against officially faulting him for malingering on the route the day Mrs. Simms' papers blanketed the neighborhood, but recommended him for a community service citation "for assisting a patron in distress." And then there were his boys. The club had met twice in the church basement and neither burned down the building nor wrecked the plumbing, so here, too, was cause for delight.

He went on. Church members who a short time before were somewhat cool toward him—probably over the melee that Sunday morning or the switch in the Sunday school hour which they didn't like or the fact that, having no acceptable alternative, they had had little choice but to vote for him as deacon—everyone, it seemed, now slapped him on the back in friendliest fashion or whispered words of encouragement. By climbing the steeple to paint the ball on top, when no one else dared, he became their hero. By tumbling head over heels from the summit and garnering assorted injuries on the way down, he earned their pity. So the paint job brought positive results to him personally, though he, in embarrassment almost to the point of shame, sloughed off the hero bit—the purple-heart status—as nothing. More on his mind, that morning's venture produced two consequences which he regretted—the paint-splotched spire, a stain upon the church that would not soon go away, and the disrepute into which the two men blamed for it had fallen. All told, his bright blue sky was not without a cloud.

He had expected a round of scolding on account of the two golden balloons that floated over the Sunday morning worship service the day after he painted the ball. "Everything I do or am connected with turns out bad," he said, scolding himself. "What kind of testimony is that? Maybe God is telling me I'm no use to Him."

He was to learn, however, that practically everyone—with the exception of the McAfees—thought mysterious balloons bursting over the heads of the congregation hilarious, and one person insisted it was the pastor's scenario to jolt the congregation awake.

But for the immediate time, the Reverend Mr. Barrett had withheld judgment. On that Sunday, after the benediction and when most of the parishioners had been greeted and were gone, he asked Luddy to explain the disruption to his sermon. To Luddy, the cause was simple.

"We have this one boy in our club who is bigger than the others," he said, offering the pastor his left hand in greeting while shielding his aching right arm. "Sometimes Will picks on the smaller boys. He did yesterday when they found the balloons in the closet."

"The ones intended for the McAfee golden wedding."

"Yep, those ones. Will grabbed the balloons away, Jamie told me last night. He's maybe our smallest kid. Lots of times he outsmarts Will. Yesterday, he wasn't going to let Will get at his balloons."

"Was he the boy with balloons tied to his wrists as he carried chairs to the choir loft?"

"That's the one. He set his chairs down, then climbed the ladder in the tower to the cubbyhole where the ventilating fan sits. He hid his balloons there."

The rest was obvious. Over the past several days work had been done on the fan—it had been out of commission for weeks.

The pastor said, "I noticed when we started the service this morning the workmen had left off the screen overlooking the sanctuary."

When the fan kicked in during the service, the balloons were picked up by the draft of air, and nature's laws did the rest.

"Why did Jamie leave his balloons up there?"

"Forgot 'em."

The pastor laughed and gave Luddy's hand an extra strong shake.

"Better see the doctor tomorrow about your right arm," he advised. And it was the next day that Luddy got his cast.

His accident on the steeple occurred in June, and here it was almost the end of July. In groups of twos and threes, and at the Ladies' Aid meeting, and choir practice, and the deacons' session before McAfee harrumphed them to order, people still talked about the carelessness of Weldon Basker and Bob Franklin, a negligence that well could have cost Luddy his life. This harsh criticism, especially of Bob, who couldn't be blamed, bothered Luddy. He didn't hold a grudge against either man, why should they? With the members, the possibility that one of their number might have died in service to his church seemed to unite the members, to help them appreciate one another more, to realize that someday some among them would step beyond the pale and whatever had been done for or against them was done unalterably, forever. But this inclusive air of brotherhood did not encompass Weldon and Bob. In fact, some people ducked out of Sunday School early to seat themselves in the sanctuary before the ushers went on duty. Others preferred that Clayton Fisher, the one of the three ushers free of controversy, seat them from his aisle. Consequently, that side of the church filled up to the impoverishment of the remaining two-thirds.

Were people being truly Christian by singling out these two men for their scorn? What did that say about Rosewood's spiritual temperature? Since he was, in a way, the cause of their censure, though escaping it, Luddy felt he should approach the pastor and plead for intercession.

In the office off the front of the sanctuary, he broached the subject to Pastor Barrett.

"I like Weldon and Bob," he said, not sure how he should phrase his concerns.

"I trust the sentiment is mutual."

"I don't want them to suffer on my account."

"I hope you'll not be suffering long on theirs."

He tried to marshal his thoughts on spirituality, on Christlikeness, on the Holy Spirit's rule in the hearts of people, and on the notion that this is what all of them at Rosewood needed. He ordered his brain to come up with appropriate words to express these thoughts. He felt only confusion, however, when on the wall he noted the pastor's seminary diploma. He scolded himself. Who was Luddy Newton? A mere layman. A layman like a hundred other laymen he was about to judge. For him to say such things to a pastor would be pretty audacious.

For several minutes more, they spoke of this and that, without an observable purpose; all the while the pastor eyed his unfinished sermon outline, and by the severest restraint tamed the urge to pick up a pencil and jot down new inspirations as they flitted through his mind. Failing to voice his convictions, Luddy instead handed Barrett his plastic bag of jawbreakers and invited him to help himself.

"The licorice are 'specially good."

Climbing the stairs to his room at the YMCA, he felt keen disappointment that he did not express what had been on his heart.

"Again, I betrayed the Lord," he said half-aloud as he took out his room key. The joy he believed he had gotten back forever had begun to slip. "At the critical moment I kept still. How can the Lord even think of using a poor failure like me?"

The visit was not entirely lost on Pastor Barrett. As soon as Luddy left he filed away his incomplete script and retrieved from a stack of papers a recent letter from a foreign pastor and laid it on his desk alongside a clean sheet. The sermon he'd preach Sunday would be about giving oneself in service to others, the universality of the Church and the importance of each member working in harmony with all other members. He had laid out his three points. Now, for filling in the details.

Since Rosewood was a Bible-believing, Bible-teaching, expository-preaching church, the substance of his message would derive from a few well-chosen Bible passages, and from the letter from Rosewood's sister church in the Dominican Republic. He picked up the letter off his desk to read it once again.

> *The work is coming along quite well, the Lord is blessing, and we are encouraged. Only in one area do we lag. The school.*
>
> *As you will remember, we are conducting classes for over a hundred youngsters in our church building, and*

when the weather permits, under the trees. For years we have challenged our people to erect a suitable building for a village school, but I am afraid the spirit of "mañana" prevails.

Do you recall that last year we suggested that you send a team of your men to the D.R. to help with a building project or two? The school is one such immediate need. I guess you would say I am pleading for such help as soon as you can organize it and send it on its way.

Odd, thought Barrett, that that rambling conversation with Luddy Newton should bring to mind the need for a school building in the Dominican Republic. He felt there was something strange about this newest deacon—how things happened unexpectedly around him. Perhaps just by being here in this office this singular fellow had started wheels in motion that might accomplish wonders in both Rosewood and in the church in the D.R.

He began the task of fleshing out his theme.

A construction crew volunteering time and talents in the Caribbean would illustrate service beyond self. A church in another culture, speaking a different language, would be indicative of the Church Universal. To be effective, his clinching point, the crew members laboring in a far reach of God's world would necessarily have to join their efforts in one harmonious whole. He would close on the note: Who will gain the greater blessing—we or they?

Focusing on the trip he would propose for the men, he lay out four motivating principles:

1. The project involves men in a cause larger than themselves.

2. They are doing something for others, with no thought of gaining something in return.

3. A team must act in concert, where all members are friends.

4. Traveling to another country presents a new environment, and staying there long enough to get the job done assures the embodiment of the first three principles.

Newton had little more than mentioned the names of the two nearly blacklisted ushers. But by mere reference to them, Barrett mused, underneath he was asking for healing of this sore in the congregation. Perhaps Luddy's unspoken plea had generated the hastily but, he felt sure, divinely guided outline before him. If this inspiration didn't end the friction between Weldon Basker and Bob Franklin and sweep away the nettles from the congregation, he was convinced nothing would, unless it be the threat of excommunication. And here at Rosewood the members didn't even know what the word meant.

Along with the rest of the assemblage on Sunday morning, Weldon and Bob, each from his own rear pew, heard Barrett's challenge to Rosewood men to roll up their sleeves and pitch in for the Lord in the needy, windswept hills of the Dominican Republic. As he greeted them in the vestibule following the service, the pastor urged first Bob, then Weldon, to become a part of the team.

"I don't know of a man more skilled in a dozen ways than you,

Bob," he said, and later paraphrased that same remark to Weldon. "I'd go so far as to say that whether this effort comes off depends to a very large degree on you."

Strange that each man asked if Luddy Newton had signed up.

"Unfortunately, Luddy can't go. His arm, you know. He'd have quite a time hammering or sawing a plank in two when his arm is still weak from the break."

Some ten men volunteered to make the three-week trip in October. Weldon and Bob, each encouraged in his own way that Luddy would not be there to haunt them, enrolled as numbers eight and nine, though Bob, number nine, sought to sign up ahead of Weldon when he learned his rival would be part of the team.

A week before their flight date, another letter came from the D.R.

> *I'm sorry to inform you that the team must delay its arrival. We haven't been able to get our building materials together —most likely will not until January. I trust your plans can hold until then. We need you, and look forward to your coming at that time.*

For those eager to undertake such a venture January came slowly, and for every man the altered plans created complications. Various team members had to apply for new vacation dates and rearrange numerous family matters. But finally the calendar turned over to the day of departure. Only one of the ten found it necessary to back out.

Luddy, who by now had shed his cast, said his arm was as good as new. He took the dropout's place.

Chapter Ten

At the lost-bags claims office in the Santo Domingo terminal, Harry Churtle tried to flag the attention of six or eight airport employees who, some appearing very official and others very unofficial, drifted in and out of the closet-sized room.

"Tools. Our tools. They no come," Harry said, struggling to make his basic English sound like the native Spanish. A shrug of the shoulders, a palms-up gesture, a shake of the head—these were the replies in universal body language.

"Where our tools?" he persisted. Having gained no satisfaction over the past fifteen minutes, he was uncertain whether to thunder, though he seldom thundered, or to throw himself on Hispanic mercy, pleading like a child for his confiscated toys. A true Anglo-Saxon with light brown hair and Teutonic flesh tones, of average height and solid build, and possessing a temperament of easy acceptance and unflappability, he nevertheless succumbed at times to mild agitation when similar circumstances drove others up the wall.

At present, he was undergoing, relatively speaking, a tantrum, a

Baltic type among Mediterraneans.

"They took our tools from us at the gate in Miami," he said, physically collaring a small, dark-skinned man with a heavy mustache who had been in and out of the claims office several times. "They said we couldn't carry them on board. I guess they didn't like hammers and saws and drills and shovels loose in the plane—or maybe they thought they were instruments for a hijacking."

"Ah, *instrumentos,*" said the man, comprehension flooding his face. "*Instrumentos americanos.*" Smiling broadly, he slipped loose of Harry's grasp and once again scuttled out through the doorway Harry turned to the one other person in the room and posed his question in a new way.

"*Instrumentos?*"

This time for a reply he received a wrinkling of a baggage handler's nose.

"Where did he go?" Harry asked his eight colleagues who stood in a rather tight circle just outside the claims office, each of them hungrily watching the retrieval of luggage by their recent fellow passengers to the Dominican Republic.

"Where did who go?" replied Weldon Basker.

"That little fellow with a mustache."

"Dime a dozen around here, I'd say," offered Bob Franklin. "What concerns me more is why our checked baggage hasn't shown up."

It soon became clear that distribution of luggage from their flight had ended. Not one article belonging to the contingent of volunteers from Rosewood Fellowship Church had been delivered.

"I'd say there may be a problem," Gilroy McAfee, head of the delegation, suggested, not wishing at this point to be overly prejudicial.

"First, our carry-on tools and now our checked things," said Weldon, who did not hesitate to judge a case either in the early stages or late. "Something fishy's going on here. That gal at the gate in Miami said they'd box up our tools and check them through on our plane."

The little man energized by the knowledge that certain *instrumentos* were evidently wayward, emerged from an office on the far side of the area and spotting Harry crossed straight to him, brimming with news.

"Instrumentos," he said, hammering in the air, followed by sawing, "Bogotá."

"Bogotá?"

"Bogotá." Having given his report, he faded away.

"Our tools were sent to Bogotá," said a subdued Harry, and nine sweating, stubbly chins drooped on shirt collars and neckties that already had begun to wilt.

Seeking information about their checked bags occupied the next twenty minutes for all nine men. Getting nowhere, they once again delegated the chore to Harry.

"Well, it will do no good to stand here," Gilroy said, bowing to reality and trying for the decisiveness required of a leader in a crisis. "Come on, men. We've got customs to go through. It's a formality in foreign travel. Our pastor should be waiting just outside."

In the customs hall, baffled agents, ready to process nine American men in conservative business suits who toted nothing, not even a shaving kit among them, asked in bewilderment if they had anything to declare.

"Are you kidding?" Bob Franklin laughed, but not with humor. "They sent our carry-on tools to Bogotá, and who knows where our suitcases are?"

"Bogotá?" The agent instructed them to wait. "Stand right there," he commanded in clear-enough English. He hurried away and after a few minutes returned with someone who, from the greater number of stripes on his uniform, appeared to be of elevated rank.

"Where your baggage?" this superior demanded.

"The building-trade tools we wished to carry with us were taken away in Miami," explained Gilroy. He realized that mason and carpenter tools hardly tallied with the suits and ties he had insisted his party wear—"For the flight we must dress our best. We *are* the Lord's ambassadors." And now in this incongruous situation he found it necessary to steel himself into calmness. "They tell us our tools have been sent to Bogotá in Colombia."

"Bogotá? Oh, that's bad," the official said.

"And who knows where our checked bags are," put in a more disturbed Weldon.

"Our bags?" called Harry Churtle, running up to join the group. "On their way to Bolivia. I finally got them to contact Miami, and they said our stuff was missent to Bolivia."

"Bolivia!" exclaimed the superior agent and his underling together. "Wait here!"

The two swept away and in through a door marked *privado*. In thirty seconds three men emerged, a new official, whose uniform sported more stripes, striding augustly ahead of the others.

"Come, come, come," he said, using all the official persuasion of his position and snapping his fingers at idle lounging agents awaiting the arrival of the next plane. Forming an inescapable phalanx, they made sure the Americans came by herding them across the now almost empty floor, down a narrow hallway, and in through an unmarked door. Their destination was a room measuring about twelve by twelve feet. Its nothingness was relieved by a single small, high window crisscrossed by iron bars but no glass, a fluorescent light overhead, and wooden benches along three walls.

"You stay," the spokesman for the third tier of customs officialdom commanded, and in Spanish imparted instructions to a big fellow he was apparently assigning as their keeper. Probably among his injunctions was one to fasten a huge deadbolt on the outside of the door, because this was the man's first undertaking.

Quiet fear ruled the cell. Fear of fire, fear of suffocating, fear of being trapped, fear that they were in a holding cell for a guillotine, a scaffold, a firing squad, or whatever the Dominicans used to eliminate unwelcome visitors. These quiet fears were kept mostly inside by each of the men, but were keenly felt nevertheless. None of the

Rosewood contingent had been out of the United States before, except to Canada, and this first experience on reaching this first foreign destination prompted them all to wonder why global travel was attractive to so many people.

"Why are they keeping us here?"

"What did we do?"

"What are they going to do to us?"

"Because somebody else lost our gear, is that any reason to turn us into prisoners?"

The questions were many, and the answers none. Some sat on the benches, a few with head in hand. Others paced the floor. Coats came off and were thrown on a heap in a corner, ties were unknotted, sleeves rolled up. Faces were mopped with soggy handkerchiefs. Harry stood on a bench but was unable to see out the window which was still a foot above his head. The roar of a plane taking off funnelled through the window and whipped from wall to wall, adding to their fears that with enough planes they'd all go deaf.

"Shouldn't we send for the American ambassador?" asked Weldon as the noise temporarily faded. His unease was beginning to turn into creative resilience. "I understand he's obliged to get his countrymen out of scrapes like we're in."

"Or else the White House threatens war," added Sherman Boyer, a firmly built fellow in his forties who himself was inclined to threaten war or at the least to skirmish when, in his opinion, any situation deteriorated.

When quiet prevailed, they heard faint sounds of snoring outside their room, and these then grew louder. Weldon pounded on the door. After the fourth battering, the snorts abruptly ceased, and their jailer pushed back the bolt and opened the door a crack.

"The ambassador," Weldon said, articulating precisely. "Take us to the ambassador."

"Bat'room?" asked the puzzled keeper. He rapped his knuckles on the door, smiled, and nodded his head. He was pleased to overcome the language gap. He couldn't have done better teaching a class of five year olds.

"Bathroom, yes, that too," Weldon agreed. "But what if you're sound asleep when we knock?" He pointed to the man, "Sleep . . you, you . . ." He then closed his own eyes and feigned a few snorts.

Catching on, their jailer knocked all the louder and kicked furiously at the door. Then in a conciliating motion, he touched his chest and with a half bow and amiable smile said, "*Yo,* Luís."

"All right, Luís, it's five minutes till noon," Weldon continued. "We're hot, hungry, and plenty burned up because your people are keeping us locked up in this cubbyhole against our will. What do you plan to do about it?"

Luís' plan was to ignore unintelligible talk, shut and bolt the door, and finish the lunch he had started to eat before falling asleep. An hour later he slid back the bolt and opened the door. He handed in a pot containing food and held out four metal plates and five spoons.

"This is all?" asked a disappointed Bob Franklin.

"The four guessing closest to the number I'm thinking of will eat first," Weldon said, accepting the government's largesse. "Three, rather, because nobody will come closer than me."

"What's in the pot?" asked a volunteer named Steve Hatfield. Ordinarily he was not real curious, but under the circumstances deemed it advisable to know how hard he should work to penetrate Weldon's mind.

"Chili, I think," said Bob Franklin, wresting one of the spoons from his rival and dipping into the pot. "Chil—"

The force of a small hurricane scattered the contents of his mouth over the floor and onto the shoes of Gilroy McAfee.

"Water! Where's water!"

Hunger then took second place to generosity as each man became willing, even eager, to let his fellow travelers eat first. Small bites would do it, testified Gilroy, who as their leader was by acclamation designated the king's taster. When too much overcome, the men pulled their handkerchiefs from their pockets to chew on, hoping by the neutrality of cotton or synthetic fibers and moisture from sweat glands to counter the fire that enflamed the roofs of their mouths, their tongues, and their gums, and was felt even down in the pits of their stomachs.

In time the pot was reasonably emptied, and kicking at the door began.

"You want—?" Luís restrained his curiosity and nodded his head toward some destination beyond the door. "Show *pasaporte.*"

"Now, don't that beat all?" thundered Bob. "I never, *ever* heard of needing a passport to go to the bathroom."

"Pasaporte," Luís said, holding out his hand.

One by one the nine dug into the breast pockets of their suit coats and turned over their passports to their jailer.

"One sure way of making us give them up," Harry said.

It was a parade through the customs hall and to the *caballeros* room on the other side. En route, for five American dollars Bob bought a Thermos from one of the passengers disgorged from an incoming flight and who stood in line awaiting inspection of his things.

Back in their detention quarters the men for the most part took to the benches. From a pocket, Harry produced a paperback novel. He had finished it on the flight from Miami and had quite forgotten he had it, but to help his fellow prisoners pass the time, split it into sections and passed it around. When it came to understanding the plot, those fortunate enough to start in the first half of the book had a definite advantage over the others. For the back-benchers, Harry recited the gist of the story, up to a particular starting point, four times.

The afternoon wore on, more slowly for some than others. A couple of the men slept. Once in a while someone kicked at the door, but it was obvious Luís was either a very sound sleeper or considered these hours as rightfully his break time.

"Any more water in that jug?" asked Bob.

"Better go slow on the water," cautioned Gilroy. "I've always heard that water in these countries can be a dangerous thing."

"Is dying of typhoid any worse than your insides bursting into flames?" countered Bob.

"I doubt you can reason with him," Weldon said to Gilroy, while nodding toward Bob. "They say when a man goes out of his head you'd better give him up."

"Huh!" humphed Bob. "When Luís opens the door I'll fill up this jug, but I think it holds only enough for eight."

"Why are they jailing us like this?" Steve asked. It was a question that had been posed every fifteen minutes all afternoon.

"Too bad Luddy's not here," Harry said. "He knows a little Spanish. He could probably find out their complaint."

"Luddy knows Spanish?" injected a doubting Weldon. "He's picked up a few words from one of his helpers on the recycling truck, but I'm afraid those kinds of words would simply land us in more trouble."

Luddy had missed the plane from Miami. He had almost missed the first leg of their flight from home. On the morning they were to leave, he sat in the parlor of the YMCA, freshly shaved and showered, shod and shined, and clad like it was Easter Sunday. He patiently listened to one of his club boys go through his list of spelling words. Only when the old and unreliable clock above the registration counter struck eight did he realize it was actually eight forty and he was supposed to have been on his way to the airport fifteen minutes earlier. Rushing to the stairway to pick up his bag and a couple of tools he was taking, he slowed just enough to accept two letters held out to him by the desk clerk. He stuffed them into his inner jacket pocket, bolted up the steps three at a time, grabbed his things, and in like manner flew down again. Giving only lip service to his usual practice of obeying the speed laws, he reached the airport and the departure gate precisely as the attendant started closing the door.

In Miami he found the gate completely closed, and through a narrow window next to the jetway saw the plane pulling away from the terminal.

He, of course, had held the same odds as his companions for making the flight over the Caribbean. But fifteen minutes before they were to board, Luddy struck up a conversation with an old gentleman who relied heavily on a cane for walking.

"We're headed for the Dominican Republic," Luddy said. "This hammer you see and this set of chisels are going to help build a school for kids there who now have to meet under a tree."

The old man listened attentively to Luddy's story. In response to Luddy's query, he said he was on his way to Los Angeles to visit his daughter and her family.

"Aren't you in the wrong departure area?" asked Luddy. "All these people are going to San Juan, and then, of course, the ten of us are continuing on to the Dominican Republic."

For Los Angeles the old man was in the wrong area. He needed to go clear to the other side of the terminal, and he had a heavy carry-on bag to lug along. Luddy picked up the bag and gently guided his newfound friend to a gate just opening to receive its

California-bound passengers.

"Sir, sir," the gate attendant called after Luddy, who had started back in a hustle to his own area. Luddy stopped and went back.

"Your father here is not on this flight. His first stop is San Juan."

"For Los Angeles?" Luddy asked, aware that they knew more about flight routes than he, but still . .

"Not California. Los Angeles, Chile—in South America," the old man said. "My daughter's husband is there on an agricultural project."

That night they shared a room in the hotel inside the Miami terminal.

The nine in confinement began to understand better their predicament when in the early evening they were ordered to completely strip and to pass their clothing out through the narrow opening allowed by Luís. They also passed their wallets and document cases out to Luís, who relayed them to an officer for inspection. These, however, were returned—"with money intact," observed a surprised Sherm Boyer.

"Drugs," said Weldon, as utterly stark as his cellmates. "They think we're into drugs."

"Me? A drug dealer?" said Steve, who had never been accused of even overtime parking. "The only drug I know is an aspirin."

"I get it," said Harry. "Bogotá and Bolivia. Suspect places everywhere. They think we sent our baggage there as a part of our running drugs."

"But drugs come *from* South America," objected Bob

"It makes no difference," countered Weldon. "We sent our bags down to be filled up for the return trip. Sending our bags down clean only confuses. A drug runner can't be too clever."

"You seem to know all the ins and outs," said Bob, a sardonic smile curling his lip.

Before midnight their clothes, except Gilroy's vest, were returned, and with them came the opportunity to take another walk through the customs room. Upon reaching their cell again, not even Luís knew where to switch off the overhead light, so they built a human pyramid and by climbing on backsides and shoulders, Sherm was able to yank the fixture free from its wires. The rest of the night passed in pitch blackness, and the more weary among them got some sleep.

In the morning it was nearly ten before they heard Luís draw back the bolt on the door. Expecting his roguish face, they were startled to see standing in the slot a grinning Luddy Newton. He was weighted down with a valise, a long, thin, bulging cardboard carton, and as many other implements used by plumbers, electricians, painters, and hod carriers as he could cradle in his arms.

"Why, Fig Newton!" exclaimed Harry Churtle. "You've been to Bogotá and back."

"Nope," replied Luddy. "Miami and San Juan. I guess you fellows forgot your tools yesterday. I found them standing in the corner next to the gate when I boarded the plane this morning."

"They let you take them on board?" asked Harry.

"Sure, why not?"

"Didn't they give you a lot of trouble?" asked Weldon.

"No," shrugged Luddy. He could think of no reason why they should.

"I told them what we were going to do with them here in the D.R., and do you know, the airline people there in Miami took up a collection and gave me sixty-five dollars to buy cement with."

And that wasn't all, he related. The tools had taken up a lot of space in the overhead compartments of the plane, so he had apologized widely for the inconvenience to other passengers.

"But when I told them we were going to build a school for poor kids in a mountain village, they sent a cup up and down the aisles, and I got thirty-seven dollars and fifteen cents. One lady said to buy pencils and paper, and maybe crayons with it."

The chief of immigration and customs, a man with much gold braid on his uniform, stood beside Luddy. Yesterday he had engineered their imprisonment. Today he swung the cell door wide open. Behind him lurked his assistant and the assistant's assistant. All three officials smiled cordially. "Contrary to reports, your instruments did not go to Bogotá," Chief Manuel Mendozo said, "and that is good. Thank you for being our guests overnight." Several who were under the impression they had been prisoners exchanged slightly cynical glances.

"You are free to go," the second in command added.

"No further inspection is needed," the last of the three said.

Men who spoke no English yesterday were rather fluent today.

"But you can't arrest us one day and treat us as scum, and the next just say, 'Goodbye, nice to have you visit.'" Sherm Boyer thought it was time for justice to prevail.

"Cool it, Sherm," cautioned Harry. But Sherm would not be cooled.

"Like the Apostle Paul told his captors, 'We're citizens of Rome—'"

"Rome?" asked the official trio's underling. "You're Italians?"

"Americans," snapped Sherm.

"But you said—"

"I said, quoting the Apostle Paul, 'We're Americans.'"

"Never mind, Sherm," others pleaded.

"What Paul said was not one of the Ten Commandments," added Harry.

"Your passports," said the middle officer, holding aloft a fistful. His quick action saved a sinking situation from deteriorating further. As he read their names, each Rosewood man accepted his precious document and with scarcely a look back quit the confining space for the openness of the customs hall.

"Basket, Weirdon Thomas."

Weldon claimed his precious little blue booklet and took a step or two into freedom.

"Franklin, Roberto Carl. Are you son of Franklin Roosevelt?"

"Churtlee, Harry Middle—Midtown, Middleton."

"Mac—Mac—MacFlee, Gib—Guy—Gibby—"

Laughter broke out. After their day of confinement, something was needed to set their minds as well as their bodies free. The mispronunciation of Gilroy McAfee's name did it.

"MacFlee!" roared Weldon Basker, whose own name had been tampered with.

"Gibby!" laughed Sherm Boyer.

"Gibby," a half-dozen among them repeated.

Gibby it would be for their time in the Dominican Republic, and when these men escorted the moniker home, its endurance could no doubt be extended considerably there, too.

One last question a few thought to ask Sr. Mendozo before they passed through the customs door and out to the world beyond.

"Our checked luggage. Where is it?"

"Bolivia."

Chapter Eleven

With nobody there to meet them, the Rosewood volunteers were on their own in a strange land. None among them, except Luddy Newton, possessed so much as a smattering of Spanish. In the past two weeks he had boned up on nouns and verbs, and now these specks of learning garnered from Carlos of his recycling collection team came in handy as the group faced what to do next.

"I thought the Reverend Juan was supposed to meet us and take us to Santa María," groused Bob Franklin. "He's nowhere around."

"That was yesterday," snapped Weldon Basker, eager to set his rival straight. "Pastors in this country have things to do besides marking time while their visitors languish in jail."

"He is a busy man," affirmed Gilroy McAfee, but in his more civil way. "After getting us squared away, he was due to go north on a preaching mission."

"You'd think he'd have left us a contact here in the city."

"Only a P.O. box number on his letters."

"So, how do we get to his village?"

"There's a Hertz sign," Luddy said, pointing to a counter at the far end of the terminal. He had paid little attention to the flare-up between the ushers, and instead searched for a solution to being stranded in foreign territory. "We can rent a van and drive ourselves out to the village."

It seemed like a good idea. Undoubtedly, they would need transportation over the next three weeks. A large van could carry them all, and perhaps at times they would remove the seats and haul supplies for building the school.

They rented the van, asked for a road map and were told there was none.

"Where you go?" asked the man behind the desk, wanting to be helpful.

"Santa María," replied three or four together.

"Santa María, *ay-ay-ay!*" The agent whacked his forehead. "Santa María—*uno, dos, tres.* Santa María del Sud, Santa María del Río, Santa María la Real de Nieva."

"*Sud,* south. *Río,* river," Luddy interpreted. "*La Real*... hmmmm, I don't know... king or queen, I think—maybe Queen of the Snow."

"Well, that one in the snow is out," said Weldon. "In all the pictures Juan has sent, I never saw any snow."

"And here we're south, on the southern coast," Sherm Boyer said. "If it were Santa María of the South, it'd have to be near the sea. I don't think it is."

"What do you say, Mr. McAfee?" asked Luddy.

"Yeah, Gibby, which of the Saint Marys do we honor with our presence?" Bob asked. Risking rebuke, he was brazen enough to be the first to use in the safety of group action the nickname they had given their leader. Gilroy did not seem to mind, or he hardly noticed. Perhaps the humor it produced after their nightmare in the lockup wormed its way into his soul and fed his desire to always be fair-minded.

"I can't refute the logic," he said, "so I suppose what's left is the town on the river."

Santa María del Río. Agreement was by consensus.

The Hertz attendant pointed in the direction they were to go, and described a few landmarks on the route out of town. He had not been there himself, he said, but if they went far enough they'd probably come across signs leading to the village.

Weldon drove, the first stick shift he'd maneuvered in thirty years. He found it fun, grinding gears, testing lights, pushing the air knob. Far from being a new vehicle, their van had a few flaws. Neither speedometer nor odometer registered, the electrical system shorted whenever he blew the horn—which was often—and he soon learned that any air introduced inside would have to blow in at the windows. Yet, what mattered these few deficiencies? He felt the power of a bus driver over his passengers, and when someone in the rear cried "Hey! Stop!" he called back that the law didn't allow unscheduled stops and kept on going, demonstrating that the accelerator worked perfectly.

"Stop," Harry Churtle pleaded. "We ought to go back and check once more on our bags."

"The airline'll send 'em out," assured Weldon, not slowing. "They do back home."

"But until they do we'll need shaving stuff and toothbrushes," reasoned Harry. "Shouldn't we stop and buy some things before leaving town?"

"By this time tomorrow, the bags'll catch up with us," Weldon said, father-like. "And if not, where we're going has to have a drug-store. *Farmacia,* they call it here, with an "F." I saw it on a store back there a ways."

With Weldon so confident, even Harry settled back to enjoy the trip.

"Good road," observed Weldon, and he pushed harder on the gas.

"But lots of poor people," said Steve Hatfield, whose feelings were attuned to any unfortunate person or animal. "Did you see those huts back there? Made out of tin."

"How do you expect to see anything the way that guy drives," groused Bob.

"Is that tobacco in that field?" Harry asked.

"Tobacco—I suppose like Cuba. Did you see those big cigars back at the airport?"

"Plenty of corn," Bob said.

"Sugar, not corn," Weldon chided. "Anyone who's been to Florida ought to recognize sugar cane."

"Look at that woman carrying a ton of stuff on her head."

"Get a load of that bus. Are those chicken crates on the roof?"

"More on top than inside."

"They must be religious people. At least there are lots of small buildings with crosses on top."

The talk rolled off Luddy. For a while he watched the unfamiliar scenes whisk by and drank in a flavorful nectar of life that until now he could only have imagined—which was only half of what he was seeing. They passed a score of overloaded buses, hundreds of houses built out of cement blocks, flattened tins, or sometimes palm leaves, each occupying a small plot, and countless numbers of families and field hands pulled up along the road to gape as the van rushed by. Other forces of recent days gradually overtook the present scene, became the stronger, and Luddy's thoughts drifted to home and to the mixed bag he had left behind.

Mostly, he thought of Meribel. She had promised to entertain the club at her house, though she was not confident the boys would enjoy the brand of M&M's offered to them—that is, Miss Moore and Meribel. She would do all right, though, Luddy believed; she'd lend to the boys a woman's touch beyond mothers and sisters that every once in a while they needed. He trusted her and was satisfied with her. But what were her feelings toward him?

He had disappointed her. Before it was determined when the volunteers would be away, or that he would be a part of them, she planned a gala party for his thirty-sixth birthday, a date she said was significant because on reaching it he would no longer be thirty-five.

When Luddy informed her he would be in the D.R. on his birthday, she was cross at first, then on Saturday night, giving way to disappointment, she cried all the way to the library.

It was all right, Luddy said, hoping to cheer her. They could celebrate at the party Mrs. Simms was giving for the three of them on the eve of his leaving.

They went, Luddy in high spirits, Meribel because going was better than staying home and letting Luddy go by himself.

They played Scrabble and Uno and old-fashioned dominoes, and Beulah rhapsodized over Luddy's innate skills. For dessert she served a lemon meringue pie. To maintain the illusion of consistency, Meribel refused the piece offered her, asking if Mrs. Simms didn't remember she was allergic to it. The hostess then urged a double portion on Luddy and treated Meribel to a fairly stale cookie from a jar purporting to be a barn owl.

On her doorstep later that night, the night of their parting, a petulant Meribel said to Luddy that it was past his bedtime and he had to get up early in the morning, so he need not come in. So there under the porch light he held her hand preparing to say good-bye, and she wept as a woman will weep when the spirit of another woman is present to season her tears with salt. Dash the light and the near certainty that neighbors spied on them from behind their curtains; he wanted to take her in his arms and say only she counted in his life. But in fifteen years he had not done this.

Yet, on this critical evening he felt he should do something, and he did. Impetuously, he kissed her on the cheek, nearly tumbled down the three steps to the sidewalk, and waved as he called on the way to his car, "Bye. See ya."

Luddy's mind was far removed, but his body occupied the van's middle seat next to the window. A sudden crisis in the drive toward their destination quickly and decisively united mental with physical, very much in the here and now. The road which Weldon had admired and to which he gave his utmost confidence abruptly changed in most of its specifications. Without warning, blacktop gave way to dirt, and it was cut with deep ruts awash from recent rains. The width of the roadway diminished and on either side in place of graveled shoulders great yawning ditches appeared. Too late for anticipation, Weldon's accelerator foot, in reaction, searched for the brake. His hand tugged at the gear shift, but because it was many years since he'd driven his old DeSoto, he forgot the necessity of engaging the clutch. The onset of danger often renders uncommon strength, and this brute force now feeding his veins, he applied to the gear lever, by sheer effort throwing it not into the lower ratio intended, but into reverse. The terrible sound of tearing metal traveled from the front of the van to the very rear.

They stopped. When the front end of a vehicle jams solidly against the far slope of a ditch, there is very little chance of going farther.

Shaken but unhurt, the Rosewood Ten stepped from the van into squishy mud, with either prayers of thanksgiving or deprecations against the driver on their lips. They stood idly looking at one another. What to do next? Luddy passed around his plastic bag of jawbreakers.

Overhead, the sun burned brightly, and here there was no place to hide from it. Shirts that hadn't been off their owners' backs for three days were soaked with sweat and grayed from grime. Hours ago neckties had been stuffed into the pockets of suit coats, which were stacked behind the third seat with the tools and the one lone bag belonging to Luddy. Pant legs and shoes were covered with mud. Gilroy McAfee's glasses had become a victim, the sudden stop sailing them off his nose and against some solid object that bent them to the fit of a conehead. No man among them said the present situation was the high point of his life.

"Where's the Thermos?" asked Sherm Boyer, poking his head inside the vehicle. "I'm about to croak."

"The Thermos?" repeated Bob Franklin, its owner. "The Thermos . . . it's back at the airport. I was so anxious to leave that prison I forgot and left it there."

"Well, if we're going to find water or get out of this ditch, we're going to have to go for help," said Gilroy, asserting command that until now had been exercised by a self-appointed surrogate, who, currently, was not in the best of graces with the passengers on his bus. "How far back was that last village?"

"Five miles, I'd say," answered Harry.

"I'll go for help," volunteered Luddy.

"I'll go with you. At least they'll have water there," Sherm said.

"Be careful about the water," Gilroy advised.

Harry, Sherm, and Luddy set off to get help. Some two hours later they returned with a farmer driving a pair of oxen. With these beasts he pulled the van out of the ditch. For payment, Luddy extracted a University of Chicago T-shirt from his bag and gave the man his choice of the remaining jawbreakers.

Filling a void, Luddy mounted the driver's seat, started up the van, grateful to find its engine still ran. The gears, however, had suffered more than shock. By slow shifting he was able to achieve first and second position, but going into high or reverse was not possible.

That this limitation on speed would be of no great consequence became apparent as each mile of the road made the preceding one seem just short of a superhighway. The hills grew into modest mountains. The road steepened and narrowed to a single track. At places, half of that was washed away. When the driving became delicate, as more frequently it did, the less brave among the passengers preferred to walk. On some inclines they were required to get out and push. To ford streams, all but the driver waded across barefoot. It was the one way they had found to gain a little relief from the heat.

For Luddy, the challenge of the road was a tonic similar to the elixir that driving the recycling truck provided five days a week at home. He missed the high seat of the truck that gave him a summit perspective on the world, and lacking were the yellow bins at curbside that were a constant reminder he served in a war to save the resources of nature. But the sight of strange trees and fields of cane, children kicking a ball just as they did back home, the dwindling road, the scorching sun, and even the chatter of the men seated behind him reminded him that they were on a mission for the Lord. All of this made Luddy glad, shoving into the deep corners of his mind the uncertainties of the situation he had left behind.

What kept the group going was the memory of a signpost they had come across an hour before. Santa María, it said, without specifying which one of the Santa Marías, lay twelve kilometers ahead. The length of a kilometer, compared to the mile, was debated until the question became moot by reason of their arrival.

The village nestled in a small, shallow valley. There may have been a hundred tiny homes. Whether one or more contained commercial enterprise was not readily discerned, but certainly nowhere was there to be seen a sign advertising a pharmacy with or without an "F." In the center of the village stood a church that, though small, dwarfed the houses. Except for scattered outbuildings, presumably for community-owned cattle, it was the only public structure in town.

It was not surprising that without fail the arrival of outsiders created a major event in Santa María. Between the time the van was sighted high up on the road and the time it had descended the mountain and entered the village, the whole population—probably six hundred people, most of which were young children—gathered in front of the church. These were the people, someone in the van remarked, that this crew would be working with, and for.

"Buenos días," Luddy, serving as spokesman for his group,

called out his window, waving and flashing his broadest grin. He jumped from the van and extended his hand to half a hundred men who sought to shake it.

Selecting elemental terms from his limited vocabulary, he established minimal communication with the people. This dented a little the language barrier between the villagers and the new arrivals, the latter of whom jabbered away in what some of the natives recognized as *Inglés*. Curious. The citizens of Santa María appeared surprised to see the *Americanos*. Not only surprised that they had come all the way from America, but that anyone would deliberately come to their village all the way from Santo Domingo.

Luddy asked where the pastor was.

The pastor? *Padre* had gone north. He might not be back for a week, two weeks, a month. By a few words and many signs Luddy explained that he and his friends had come to build a school for their children.

This news made them ecstatic. How long they had waited for this day! Grateful women rushed to bring them food. Men showed them where in the back room of the church they could lay out their sleeping bags. Except that they had no sleeping bags. Well, then, the villagers would lend them their own straw mattresses and blankets. By this time all among the Rosewood Ten realized Santa María had no Marriott or Hilton—or even a Motel 6.

Chapter Twelve

"There are varmints in these straw mattresses," Harry Churtle said, greeting his roommates as they started their first full day in Santa María. He spoke with neither complaint nor surprise, but merely presented a practical alternative to "good morning."

"Varmints? You mean bedbugs and lice and stuff?" asked Bob Franklin, who would recite a litany of his ailments if you merely asked the usual "how're you?" He rubbed just short of scratching a colony of small blisters streaked across his stomach. "They mistook me for the main course at their annual banquet."

This triggered a contest to top his night of woe. So much for Harry's placid start to the day. "I didn't sleep a wink," growled Weldon Basker.

"Then that musta been a snoring rat in your bed," Bob said, scoring first in the ushers' daily duel.

"Nothing wrong with a straw mattress. If it's good enough for the have-nots, the haves should expect no better. Among these victims of First World bigotry, I expected straw mattresses." This from

Keith Lawrence, a college student who with consummate idealism had sacrificed a semester so in this three-week mission he might conquer world poverty and ignorance.

"No straw tick for me. Yeachhhhh!" shuddered Thad Johnson, a balding, somewhat flabby middle-ager. "It was safest to sleep directly on the concrete."

Except for Luddy, the substitute, he was the last to sign up for the trip. For weeks he kept changing his mind; he wanted to help build the school, but instinct told him trouble started fifty miles from home, in any direction. To go to the Dominican Republic in the middle of the Caribbean was to plunge over the edge of the earth. Possessing a squeamish stomach, he had eaten very little of what the women had offered last night, choosing rather to endure cramping hunger pangs, which were relieved only partially and temporarily by one of Luddy's jawbreakers. Fearful that the bedding loaned to him had not been freshly laundered, he wiped the floor with the blankets, deposited them outside, then guardedly lay down on the clean patch, using his suit jacket for a covering, his shoes for a pillow.

"*You* can do it. You've got the padding," Harry said, being more honest than unkind.

Built-in cushioning or not, this morning Thad's stiff joints challenged his yen for cleanliness. "I thought I felt a snake crawling in my straw," said Steve Hatfield, the incurious, quiet one.

"But you didn't get up to find out."

"No. In case it was a snake, I gave him half the bed."

"I'm glad you kept your mouth shut," Thad said, "or I'd a been out that door in one leap."

The amassing chronicle continued during the time-sharing of Luddy's razor by half the men, the others exulting in their freedom at last to grow beards. The decent beds and minimal conveniences they had anticipated but lacked were blamed on the absent pastor. What kind of host would leave them alone among people who were not expecting them, with no one to adequately bridge the language gap? And because they were not expected, the villagers, with nothing planned and nothing better to offer, put them up in this room. It obviously was a place to store cast-off church accoutrements, and judging from the debris they'd swept out and the odor that clung despite the sweeping, it had served in the recent past as a shelter for some type of domesticated animals.

The pastor's house stood across the street from the church. A duplicate of the other small homes in the village, it was built of rough, unpainted lumber and had a rusty corrugated metal roof. It differed from the others in that someone had nourished a couple of struggling bushes on either side of the door, and curtains of faded cloth hung at the windows. A heavy padlock secured the entry. What kind of a man was this pastor who lived there?

"It's a Catholic church, so he must be of that denomination," Harry reasoned.

"It's Catholic, all right," Thad said. "I peeked in last night and saw the place was full of statues and candles."

"When I went to get water for shaving this morning, I met three or four women heading for the church. I guess something goes on whether the pastor's in town or not."

"Call him a pastor if you want. He's a priest."

"Our church supporting a Roman priest?" Weldon shook his head in disbelief.

"Maybe he's Protestant and trying to convert them," suggested Steve.

"Yeah," added Bob. "Sort of under cover until he can win 'em over."

There was general agreement that such was the case. At no time during the previous evening, however, had any parishioner stepped forward to declare himself the first convert.

Sherman Boyer had heard enough about flea bites and buzzing mosquitoes and aching muscles and sentient nightmares and absent pastors and church statues and candles.

"When do we eat?" he demanded.

"*What* do we eat?" amended Weldon.

Gilroy McAfee sensed that every man in the room was looking at him and felt that most threw blame his way. He realized that as leader of this crew he should not have permitted Weldon to spirit them out of the city until they had stocked up on food and other necessities. They had nothing, not even scraps from the feast with which the villagers had feted them last evening. This uncertainty of how they would be fed was another hardship of a missing host.

"I know nothing more about what we'll eat than you men do," he confessed.

At that moment someone kicked at the door from the outside. Young Lawrence opened it. Luddy, his arms laden with fruit and bread, flashed a grin.

"Hope you all like mangoes and papaya," he said. "And bread just out of the oven."

Several of the men carried pocket knives, so fell to carving and slicing. They made quick work of Luddy's bounty, but none quicker than the starving Thad. Gilroy, amazed at the instant answer to a prayer he'd had no time to utter, said before doing anything else they should conduct morning devotions. Luddy, the only one to have a bag, was the sole possessor of a Bible.

"It's a modern version," he warned. He then read from John's Gospel.

"'There are many homes up there where my Father lives . . .'"

"Is that what it says?" interrupted Weldon, doubt saturating his question.

"Yep. '. . . and I am going to prepare them for your coming. When everything is ready, then I will come and get you, so that you can always be with me where I am. If this weren't so, I would tell you plainly.'"

"In the real Bible it says 'mansions.'"

"Yeah, Weldon," rebutted Sherm, "but how can there be a lot of mansions inside a house, as we've always read it?"

"Don't forget, with God anything is possible."

"But a mansion is a big house. And a house containing many big houses?"

"What Luddy read makes sense to me," said Harry.

"Me, too," added Steve Hatfield. "How does the Twenty-third Psalm read, Luddy?"

He flipped to it.

"'Because the Lord is my Shepherd, I have everything I need! He lets me rest in the meadow grass and leads me beside the quiet streams.'"

"That's really clear," Harry declared. "No 'shall not want'—which means what?"

"Any but the most pig-headed . . ." added Bob, and very slightly dropped his head toward Weldon, " . . . has to say Luddy's new version is crystal clear as a bell."

Gilroy, the fair diplomat, cut in to say it was time to pray. He expressed thanks for the plain language they had heard—and in doing so got rather mixed up trying to match the Elizabethan endings of his verbs to the thees and thous with which he seeded his prayer.

In scrounging for their breakfast, Luddy had come across the land the villagers had set aside years before for a school. It needed clearing of brush and leveling, but on it a pile of rocks had grown over a long time. A mound of sand sat nearby. These were the only resources assembled, causing Luddy to think it strange that the earlier date for starting the project had been postponed until now, and sand and rocks were all that could justify the delay.

"We can ready the site and dig footings this morning," he said, regaining his usual optimism. "And maybe tomorrow we can turn up more materials to work with."

"Do you have the building plan?" Gilroy asked Thurston Biddle, who, though not an architect, was a meticulous draftsman for an architectural firm. Under the tutelage of one of the partners, he had drawn up a sketch to guide them in their construction.

"Right here," Thurston replied, and brought from the breast pocket of his suit coat a folded set of papers that was to govern their activity over the next three weeks.

"Good," Gilroy said. "I was afraid it went to Bolivia with your luggage."

"Not *this* sweet paper."

The next item to be considered was clothing. Luddy wore the jeans and T-shirt he had carried aboard the plane in his hand luggage. The others had only their Sunday suits, worn for the journey by command of Gilroy McAfee—hence, through imprisonment, car wreck, and a troubled night—the only threads in their possession. By this time, these suits resembled more the duds of a rescue mission's patrons than of suburbanites who wore them to a most respectable church every Sunday.

"How can I dig a ditch in my good suit?" asked Bob. "My wife picked this out, and she'll kill me when I get home."

"Better pick your funeral hymns now," Weldon said. "It already looks like a garbage collector's at the end of the day. No offense, Luddy."

Since he was a recycler, not a garbageman, Luddy did not consider himself the butt of Weldon's humor. Ignoring him, he told the group how to solve their problem.

"Trade clothes with men in the village. They've got work clothes. Maybe that's all they've got. They'll probably love to wear your suits to church on Sunday."

"And go home in jeans or cut-offs?"

"Trade back before we leave. You'll both get a good wear from the trade, so it should be no problem."

They found no reluctance among the village men to exchange their rough, casual wear fitting for the task ahead, for suits and what once were dress shirts. But before Thad's new clothes could be washed and dried in the sun, a requisite if he were to put on someone else's clothes, and before Thurston could stretch out his strings to mark the trench for the footings of the new building, a delegation of the locals approached the school site where the Americans had gathered and complained they had been cheated.

Luddy huddled with the dissatisfied citizens, and going back to his colleagues said:

"They want your neckties, too."

This minor tear in the relationship mended, the villagers and their visitors got along very well. Gilroy, through Luddy's elementary Spanish, asked for help in constructing the school. Probably more would have volunteered had they understood the question, and more still if pesos had been mentioned. But even with the intent of the American chief's words still mostly a mystery, a dozen men stepped forward. The international, intercultural, interfaith team that soon formed made good progress the first day. Villagers who did not take turns digging or grubbing bushes or cutting down a small hill, stopped by frequently to check out the job or to carry on one-sided conversations with the *Americanos*. Luddy whistled, and his colleagues also whistled or sang as they worked. The misfortunes that had marked their stay in the D.R. up to this point were tossed away with each shovelful of dirt. The atmosphere changed. Even Weldon and Bob, the rival ushers, seemed to have muted their feud.

The Americans were not without talent. Thurston had tagged along on enough construction site visits with the architects in his firm that he was looked to as project coordinator. Weldon had once laid a new floor in his garage and brought along a couple of trowels he'd used on that job. Sherman and Bob contributed brawn to the group's assets. Luddy had several skills—none matching a journeyman's, but those of an eager apprentice.

Pablo, Jorge, Francisco, Bernabé, and William, among others, were willing hands. Before the day ended, enough banter and little acts of goodwill took place that both villagers and visitors knew the benefits to come from their work would be more than just a building.

True, the Americans had to admit they were soft, and neither toughening of body nor of emotions would occur overnight. But blisters were overlooked to the extent possible, and use of a common tin cup to dip water from a clay pot increased in proportion to the heat of the day. Even Gilroy took his turn scooping up the cool, refreshing thirst quencher, and after skimming off the surface, Thad closed his eyes and pretended he was drinking from the ice-water tap in the door of his refrigerator back home.

Site clearance and the trench for the footings took longer than anticipated. For three days they worked on these backbreaking jobs. They were reconciled to knocking off at noon for lack of materials, and glad for the break, when Luddy and Thurston drove up in the debilitated van with two dozen bags of cement. They had found a "real town" some two hours away by a road proportionate to the transmission limitations of the van.

"We'll get more cement tomorrow, and the rods we need, and a bunch of stuff. I've still got money from the collection by the airline people."

Out of gratitude for their contribution to the village's welfare, the women provided meals to the Americans. Each day more local men gave over their cattle duties to others and helped with the construction. While the team worked under Thurston's supervision, mixing the cement and pouring the school's foundation and floor,

Luddy, accompanied by Harry one day and Sherm another, delivered new materials. Then one day a large truck descended into the valley. It carried tons of brick. Luddy was expecting concrete blocks. In this purchase, the Spanish lesson by Carlos back home had not covered the appropriate nouns.

So instead of a three-room gray-block school house, Santa María would have a three-room school of red brick. Who knew? It might become the distinction setting this village apart from all others around.

The workmen experimented with various textures of mortar, one of the villagers mixing the mud that best held the bricks together. The courses mounted slowly, row upon row, some laid neatly and straight, some a bit too haphazard had there been an exacting inspector. Ten days into the project, the walls were up, open spaces left for doors and windows. The next task was the roof. No one among the Rosewood Ten or the village men had ever built a roof like the school required.

"Make it flat, that's easiest," advocated Weldon.

"Of course not," countered Bob. "How do you expect a flat roof to bear up in the weather?"

"You're speaking of a snowstorm?" Weldon asked cynically. "You think this is Santa María, Queen of the Snow?"

The dilemma of how to construct a suitable roof ended the day Luddy returned to the village after scouting a wide area around. He brought a carpenter.

"Have you ever built a roof?" Gilroy tried to ask, though in pushing his newly acquired Spanish beyond his ability he confused cellar with roof.

"It's his specialty," Luddy said. "Roofs, not basements."

The crew was sorting out assembled lumber to begin the roof one morning when a car was sighted working its way slowly and carefully down the mountain into the valley. As usual, people gathered in front of the church—the Americans among them—to await the arrival of an outsider.

"Maybe it's the pastor returning?" suggested Harry Churtle.

"*Pastor? Non,*" replied a villager who picked up on a word familiar to both languages. Evidently, the village pastor did not drive so fine a car.

In a few minutes the vehicle arrived, and many hands reached to open the driver's door. A man got out. He was not known to the villagers, but the Americans recognized him.

"Sr. Mendozo!" a half-dozen exclaimed.

The chief officer of airport customs and immigration stood before them, in full uniform, the gold stripes on his sleeve flashing in the bright sun. Wearing the same stern face that the Americans had encountered on arriving at the airport less than two weeks before, he acknowledged no greeting in English or Spanish. He did not advance his hand toward anyone.

"I suppose you brought us our bags? The ones that went to Bolivia?" asked Sherm Boyer, breaking the silence.

"No," replied Manuel Mendozo and continued in perfectly understood English. "Your bags, if they ever arrive, will be confiscated as evidence. In my pocket I have warrants for the arrest of nine suspected drug dealers."

Chapter Thirteen

"Why just nine?" demanded Weldon Basker. "There are ten of us."

Mendozo pointed to Luddy.

"He is okay. Good man. He brought your tools. Proved you were not drug dealers."

"So if they proved we're not, why are you saying now we are?"

"The cold bottle. What do you call it? Termos?"

"That was yours, Bob," said Sherman, leveling a finger at the Thermos' owner.

"You all drank from it," Bob replied.

"Sr. Mendozo, why does a Thermos bottle containing water from the airport's faucet give you cause to charge us as drug dealers?" asked Gilroy McAfee, appealing to the reasoning he presumed any government official was capable of exercising.

"Heroin," answered Mendozo. "We found the Termos in the room you *Americanos* occupied overnight as guests of the government."

"Prisoners," corrected Weldon.

"So what if we left the bottle behind?" Bob said. "I forgot it."

"Yeah, what's it got to do with drugs?" Harry wanted to know.

"We took it apart," Mendozo informed them. "Between the glass liner and the outer casing we found heroin. Or maybe it was cocaine."

"Bob Franklin, now you've done it," Weldon charged. "Why didn't you look the thing over before you bought it?"

"We were thirsty, that's why. Remember? You couldn't wait for your turn at it."

The villagers pressed around the gold-braided official and the men who for some ten days had been building their school. The words in English held no meaning for them, though from the tones with which each side spoke they knew the confrontation was no happy meeting. They wondered why the official had sought out the Americans and how his coming would affect their friends. What fate Mendozo had in mind for them also interested the Americans.

"What are you going to do, Sr. Mendozo?" asked Luddy. "Take them all back to town?"

"Not now," the officer answered. "Today, I arrest. Another day I come with a bus."

"You're not going to hole us up in that little room with the wood benches at the airport, are you?" Thad Johnson was just getting used to sleeping on a bed of sand he had constructed in one corner of the church storage area.

"Not the airport. The jail."

"We've got a school to finish," objected Sherm. "How can we put the roof on if you throw us in jail?"

"*Americanos,*" shrugged Mendozo, "they find ways."

"Is your jail a modern one, approved by Amnesty International?" asked Keith Lawrence. In the week he'd lived the more primitive life, the collegian spoke less about injustices heaped on the Dominicans and felt more the inconveniences he had to endure. Mendozo laughed as he said the jail had been built by Columbus.

"How did you find us?" Luddy wanted to know. Not being enmeshed in Mendozo's net, his curiosity could range further than the anticipation of bodily comforts or the lack of them.

"You rented a van," Mendozo said. "Did you not expect us to know that? You asked the Hertz agent for directions to Santa María del Río. I went to del Río, but you were not there."

"We weren't?" Weldon was surprised.

"So I went to Santa María del Sur. You had been expected, but did not arrive. The people there had gathered materials for the school they said you were to build. They had plans to take you into their homes."

The Rosewood men exchanged puzzled looks.

"So there was only one more Santa María—"

"Queen of the Snow!" said Weldon.

"Santa María la Real de Nieva."

"You mean we've been building in the wrong village?" asked Thurston.

"That explains everything," Gilroy said.

"Everything, Gibby, but what we're going to do now," Bob Franklin said.

"I will tell you what you are going to do," said Mendozo. "Until I return, you are prisoners of the citizens of this village." He scanned the throng of local Dominicans, all of them cowed by the stern look that, coupled with the uniform, seemed to certify his authority over them. In Spanish, the customs officer asked, "Who is the head man here?"

Relieved that collective disquiet could be shunted onto one man, the villagers turned to Bernabé, some pointing to him and others calling out his name. He stepped forward. A man of about fifty, solidly built, capable of a quick smile, he led by quiet example in his large family and in the village. A practical man, he submitted to authority when it clearly was necessary, and when it was prudent to do so, he and his fellow villagers superseded national policy by strictly local practices. At this point, he recognized that compliance was called for.

"You are Bernabé?" the officer asked in Spanish.

Bernabé nodded.

"Bernabé, you are to keep the *Americanos* under guard at all times. Understand?"

Again, he nodded.

"The government holds you responsible until these men can be taken to Santo Domingo to pay for their crimes."

Mendozo stretched his arm toward Bernabé and ran his index finger fully across the chief's throat. Bernabé understood his meaning. So did the Americans and the villagers.

For the rest of the day the Americans, except for Luddy, were kept in their dormitory at the rear of the church. Two guards posted by Bernabé sat on either side of the door. Unarmed, they chatted congenially with the prisoners who stood in the open doorway, and other villagers flocked around the makeshift prison's two windows, hoping to understand just a little why these open-hearted Americans had, by the brief visit of an official in a gold-garnished uniform, become objects of government displeasure.

"Who will finish our school?" they asked one another.

It was also a question that in the shade of his house Bernabé put to the free-roaming Luddy.

"Who'll finish the school?" Luddy repeated. "We will."

The village head man understood Luddy to have said the Americans now confined to the church storage room would complete the task they had started. It baffled him.

"Sure, why not?" said Luddy, and the confidence with which he spoke would have been convincing in any language. "Mendozo said to keep our men under guard. He didn't say where they had to be kept."

The following morning work on the roof resumed, and the volunteer helpers among the village men doubled. Two old men were assigned surveillance of the road that wound down the mountain and into the village. Should a vehicle show, they were to sound an alarm and the Americans would be hustled back to confinement. None appeared, however, and the work went on. That evening the first of what would be several community celebrations took place in the clearing in front of the church—completion of the school was in sight. Following a meal of beef and beans, singing and dancing began, aided by one man's saxophone and another's drum. The government wards and their jailers joined together in happy coexistence, each striving to use the other's language. Only Gilroy McAfee stood to one side, not sure this was what he had left home for. Yet, not far into the evening he caught himself foot-tapping and, finding it impossible to control, relaxed and let a smile turn up just slightly the very ends of his mouth.

When the children grew sleepy and the adults began to tire, Luddy retrieved his Bible from the room at the back of the church. He held it up for all to see, then read a passage from the New Testament.

"Niño . . . malo. Muchacho . . . malo," he said several times, and the villagers presumed he had read about a naughty boy. Only after much pantomime did they grasp it was the Prodigal Son. A woman familiar with the story's details then told it in Spanish to the crowd, and at its conclusion they applauded. The Americans retired to their prison, and the guards resumed their posts on either side of the door. The windows became handy exits for anyone who wished to go in or out and did not want to cause an ethical problem for their keepers.

Only the metal sheathing remained to be installed. Luddy had delivered one load. On the morning of his thirty-sixth birthday, he drove off to get another, traveling now without Thurston, the project coordinator, because Mendozo could return any time and make a head count of the nine he had arrested. Luddy's goal was the town of Repisa, up and over the mountains that walled in the valley, and farther inland, lying in the opposite direction from which most visitors came to Santa María—that is, the few who came to this tiny dot on the map. If the more-traveled road to the south was scarcely passable, the trail he would follow today was trying even to horses and ox carts. Second gear was the most the van was capable of, and it was the most that would be called for today. On one of his previous trips for building supplies, Luddy had been told about Repisa. It was a town of some significance, situated on a rather main route linking the country's north and south coasts. He could get all the tin he needed, and indeed, hauling it was his only problem. But his load today should suffice. This, he figured, would be his final trip.

Luddy's absence allowed Harry to plan a party for his friend. Leaving the construction to the others, he busied himself by conferring with the women about special food and purchasing a variety of trinkets from the villagers so each of Luddy's colleagues would have a present to give him. Luddy had said nothing about his birthday and perhaps had forgotten it was today, but Harry remembered. At the airport back home, he'd promised Meribel he would throw a party and tell everyone he was doing it in her behalf.

Work slowed as the crew used up the available material. Luddy had said he'd be back by noon, but they ate their lunch, and most bowed to the local custom of a siesta after eating. By mid-afternoon Luddy and the van and the roofing had still not returned.

Squatting in the shade outside their room, much as the village men squatted in the shade of their houses, several of the Americans conversed idly among themselves.

"Why do they call this place Queen of the Snow?" Weldon asked.

"Who knows? Those mountains around us, let alone the valley, never saw snow in their lives."

"My question is," Bob Franklin began, "how did you get off track, Weldon, and lead us here instead of to Santa María del Sud where we ought to have gone?"

"Luddy drove part of the way, too," Weldon said in self-defense. "But all the forks and side roads came before we hit the ditch."

"Maybe God wanted these people here to have a school instead of the ones we planned on building for," Sherm Boyer offered. "What do you think, Gibby?"

"That's possible."

"God's will and Weldon's mistake," cut in Bob, and his laugh was somewhat cynical.

Harry approached the small cluster of men and squatted beside them.

"We're all set for tonight. I just hope Luddy gets back in time."

"Hardly seems fair that he goes scot-free while we all face drug charges and, who knows, maybe years rotting away in a dark, damp cell for a crime we wouldn't even know how to commit." In this idle time not only Weldon, but each of the nine accused, had had time to ponder their fate, and what they foresaw was not a pleasant prospect.

"Luddy's free because he wasn't with us when Bob bought that confounded Thermos," said Thad Johnson, and his knees unable any longer to sustain a squat, he flopped to the ground, leaned against the building, stretched out his legs, and wiped his face with an already soaked handkerchief.

"Luddy got us out from under arrest before," remarked Steve Hatfield, who in the last couple of days had said even less than he usually did. "Maybe he can pull something again."

"He's helped out a lot on this project, like he always knows what to do, how to find and bargain for materials, cheering us up." Thurston Biddle's appraisal of their de facto leader was not without a limitation. "But don't expect him to pull off a miracle again."

"Luddy can afford to be cheerful," said Weldon. "Simply because he missed the plane in Miami and arrived after we were already tagged as dope peddlers."

"If Fig were being strapped in the electric chair," rebutted Harry, "he'd come up with something to lighten the heart of his executioner. Don't ask me his secret. It's just there."

Maybe Luddy did have something to offer their friendship, Harry thought in a sort of self-convicting voice to himself. Not just to benefit him, but the others as well. Not something you could put your finger on, not like on the several occasions Harry had enumerated, but something to make you feel good, perhaps to set your spirit free when the rest of you were being held a prisoner.

"This trip has transformed . . . Luddy," said Thurston, having meant to say "us."

"It started when he became a deacon," Bob said.

"I guess becoming the people's choice made him a new man," added Harry.

"That and being in the wrong place at the right time, such as at Miami with the gate closed."

"And knowing a few key words of Spanish."

Several times in the waning afternoon the men strolled to the school site and invariably commented that one more load of roofing metal would complete the job. But where was that load? Where was Luddy? Time was running out. Not just today's daylight, but their stay in this village—either by Manuel Mendozo's order or by the airline flight schedule they once had no question about meeting. The sun sank behind the western rim of the mountains, and as darkness quickly settled on the valley, the villagers brought out their lamps and flares for another celebration—this one to especially mark the birthday of "the lively one." But he did not appear.

"Start the meal," Harry said, disappointed by the absence of the guest of honor.

Start they did, and finish. They also started and finished the games Harry had planned, as well as the usual singing and dancing. And to carry on Luddy's introduction of Scripture reading into their evening of friendly fellowship, Gilroy read about the death of Jesus on the cross and his resurrection three days later. The woman among the villagers most familiar with the Bible retold it in Spanish.

"Where is he?" Sherm asked after the Americans had returned to their room. "You'd think he'd be considerate enough to get home for his own party."

"He didn't know it was coming off," said Harry.

"Maybe he got the van in a tight spot and couldn't get out," said Bob. "Remember that from Weldon's smashing it into a ditch it won't go in reverse."

About an hour after the festivities ended, the whole village heard him ease down the mountain in second gear. By the time he arrived, all had reassembled in front of the church.

Luddy hopped from the driver's seat and nodded when several men offered to pull the metal sheets from the rear of the van. Luddy crossed in front of the vehicle and opening the door on the passenger's side, reached in to take something from the front seat. At that instant, the cry of a very young baby was heard. It came from the bundle of blankets Luddy cradled in his arms.

"A baby? You brought back a baby?" asked Weldon, almost beside himself in disbelief.

"A baby girl," Luddy said, the wide grin on his face caught in the beam of someone's flashlight as he partially unwrapped his bundle. "I want you all to meet Felicité."

Chapter Fourteen

Felicité cried because she was hungry.

A new mother in the crowd recognized the complaint and, handing her own infant to her husband, took the strange baby from Luddy's arms and nestled it to her breast.

"That's what she wanted," Luddy said, pleased beyond measure to find a surrogate mother who did not have to be asked. "I had these two bottles of baby formula from Repisa and a diaper, but when the bottles got empty and the diaper full, I wondered if Felicité and I would ever make it to Santa María. But here we are, home among her daddies."

"Her daddies?" Keith Lawrence, the collegian, asked but got no answer.

Gilroy McAfee posed a more penetrating question, "But, why?"

He perhaps spoke for the other men in their guarded room after the baby had been fed, the crowd dispersed, and Luddy had constructed a bed for Felicité out of old cement bags and the blankets he had brought her in. She slept contentedly, indifferent to having had no known father and now about to inherit ten fathers.

"Why did you bring this baby here—to us?"

"Why? Well . . . I had to."

There was an explanation, but he was not certain how to begin it.

"If we'd been here nine months, I could understand why you had to," said Weldon. "But two weeks? Even for a fellow as go-go as you are, there's a limit to what you can do in two weeks."

"No, no," Luddy said, sure that his blush glowed in the dark. "It's not like that."

"Then what is it like?" Bob Franklin asked.

"Well, you all know I go to Repisa to get metal roofing. The other day on my first trip, there was this young woman—this girl, maybe fifteen, sixteen—hanging around the yard where they sell the roofing. She asked me to hold her baby for a minute while she went next door to get the tyke's bottle. I did, and the baby cooed real cute. "'She likes you,' the mother said.

"'And today the girl was there again with the baby—Felicité, she said her name was—and asked me to hold her just like the other day. I did, but the girl didn't come back and didn't come back, so finally one of the men at the yard went next door to get her.

"'She's gone,' he said, 'and the baby is yours.'

"'Yours? You mean mine?' I said. 'What do you mean, mine?'

"'The old woman who lives in the house said the girl ran off and that you are to take the baby and keep her.'

"'But that's impossible!' I said."

"Maybe you misunderstood their Spanish," Sherm Boyer suggested.

"No, the guys in the yard spoke some English. I guess the mother was too poor to raise the child, so she thought I was a rich American who could."

"Was she a . . . a . . . you know . . ." asked Weldon.

"I don't know anything about her," replied Luddy. "But if she was a . . . a . . . one of those women, I wouldn't hold it against the baby."

He said the owner of the supply yard, the husband of the old woman next door, seemed to be a pretty wise old man—"and I heard he's the mayor, too"—and when he said Luddy should take the baby, that's when he decided he would.

"'It's the mother's will,' he said, 'and God's will.' So if it's God's will, how could I not take her?"

"And what do you propose to do with this gift from God?" asked Gilroy, who never allowed his view of the end to be obscured by the means to achieve it.

His was a question Luddy was not yet ready to answer, except to say, "I guess it's up to us." The inclusion of his audience did not immediately hit home with them.

Throughout the night he lay close to the tiny bundle, listening like a new parent for the infant's breathing and ready to pop a freshly filled bottle in her mouth should she awake. Lying there for long hours without sleep, he decided it was not fair to saddle his colleagues with a next-to-newborn whose tiny dark face and abundance of jet-black hair were all that any of them had yet seen of her. And how could he, without a wife, pretend to parent this little one? Oh, the mechanics he probably could do. He'd purchased a carton of formula, the last on the shelves in Repisa, and soon would pick up more diapers in Santo Domingo. But a baby girl needed more than formula and diapers. Yet how could he know what she needed? He had to be realistic. Resolving to be, he began to phrase in many ways how he would ask this one or that one in the village here to give Felicité a home.

At dawn, he sat outside next to the sleeping guards and fed a fresh bottle to the tiny girl. He was amused by the tireless little jaws, pumping in a steady rhythm, though periodically releasing her grip on the nipple and allowing a stream of bubbles to flow with a hiss into the bottle. Each time, she popped open her eyes. She seemed to look directly at him, as if to signal that bonding had begun. He wasn't sure whether to relish these brief glimpses into her soul, or to be afraid for the little one's future.

The village began to stir, and in the next several minutes, before the sun had shown through a dip in the mountainous ring to the east, six or eight persons came by to peek at Luddy's prize.

"You take to America, *non?*" said a young man in fractured English. He lived on the far side of the village and rose early every morning to drive his herd to pasture on the mountain range. This morning, however, he detoured from his usual route in the hope of glimpsing the lively one with his new daughter.

"Niña," said an old granny, pleased that she could educate this stranger in what he now possessed.

While his fellow team members nailed on the last pieces of roofing and finished up other little jobs on the school, Luddy watched over the baby, heard a lot of advice of which he comprehended little, and in pairing the few Spanish nouns and verbs he knew, asked a number of men and women if they would take Felicité into their homes. None said they would, and this he put down to his inability to communicate.

Their three weeks in the Dominican Republic would in a day or two end. They had built a school, which was their purpose in coming. But didn't they have a larger purpose, a more significant aim in their contact with these people? Luddy felt he did. Clumsily he had tried; he'd read to them about Jesus. But did they understand any of it? What Jesus meant to him, he couldn't explain. It was the same story over again. Whether in Spanish here or at home in his native English, he could never seem to articulate the convictions that drove him. He felt inadequate, sometimes an utter failure. Would they—he—leave Santa María with a school building, but with nothing beyond bricks and a tin roof? Was this leanness in ministry due only to language? By driving away from Repisa with Felicité on the front seat, had he not clearly promised the people there he would be responsible for this child? So why was he trying to give her away to those who obviously did not want her?

On the roof of the school, in the three rooms into which it was divided, and in the yard surrounding it, the Rosewood volunteers talked as they cut and hammered and swept and raked. Four conversations were going, but only one topic: The Baby.

"Fig seems a natural when it comes to the father role," said Harry. He looked down from the top of a ladder to four or five men below.

"Fathering? Better him than me," Weldon said. "I've had my brood."

"What does he know about the kid's background, her parents, her genes?" asked Bob.

"Just that she's a tiny human being," Steve Hatfield added. He gathered up the tools they'd take to the States. "If Shirley and I didn't have an infant ourselves, I'd be tempted to take her home."

"Can a baby born in this climate live through a winter of snow and ice?" asked Thad Johnson, assuming her dark tones were an irreversible stamp of the tropics. "I'd be afraid she'd get sick or die, and I'd get the blame."

"What about you, Gibby?" asked Sherm. "Do you think we ought to carry this child off to the States?"

After a pause appropriate to his usual review of a situation, Gilroy answered, "Well, I suppose there's something to be said on either side. Separated from her own people—that might not be good. But raised in a Christian home in America would certainly be advantageous."

"She's already separated from her people," Harry argued. "Her mother ran out on her. What greater separation can there be?"

By noon the last nail had been driven, the rooms swept out, the tools bundled together; the project was finished. Returning home was now on the minds of the men. Lunch over, they lounged on their straw mats in what some called their dorm and others their prison.

"I don't want to be a wet blanket," said Thurston, knowing he was. None among them was more logical than this architectural draftsman. "In thinking about going home, you mustn't forget we're prisoners of the Dominican government."

"And that our plane leaves tomorrow night, with or without us."

"Nontransferable tickets."

"The people here won't stand in the way of our leaving," Luddy said. "I've talked with Bernabé. He reminded me they're unarmed. Says they'd be powerless if we decided to escape."

"It'd be simple to get away if you hadn't complicated things, Luddy, by bringing that baby here." Weldon shook his head, sighting disaster in Luddy's thoughtlessness.

"She won't take up much room," Luddy assured him. "I'll hold her on my lap."

"But you can't just take a baby out of the country without papers. Think of the stink *that* would raise. If Mendozo gets his way, they'll hang us for drug dealing. But for you, it'll be the rack for kidnapping."

"I've tried and I can't get anyone here to accept Felicité," Luddy said, biting his lower lip and shaking his head in resignation. This being fact, some decision had to be made. He felt it was not his prerogative, but he'd sort of put it to a vote.

"Do we want to take her home with us?"

"As your baby?" asked Sherm.

"He once called us all her daddies," Thad remembered.

"Why," said Luddy, "I thought maybe the church could adopt her."

"The church?"

"You mean the whole Rosewood Fellowship Church?"

"Sure. There must be a dozen families back home who would be willing to raise her."

"A dozen mamas and papas sound like trouble to me," said Weldon.

"Only one set of parents at a time. Maybe for six months running. When she gets old enough she can decide for herself who she wants to live with."

"Under the circumstances, sounds reasonable to me," Harry said.

"Me, too," agreed Thurston.

"I'm against it," Weldon barked.

"So am I." Bob seemed surprised he was agreeing with Weldon. "What do you say, Gibby?"

Luddy feared Gilroy's answer. Glancing at him, he saw that his face was burdened with a frown. If anything, Gilroy McAfee was a practical man. He looked before leaping. If in doubt, don't. He deplored mopping up spilled milk. Luddy had to admit even to himself that in his hopes for this baby there were far more questions than answers.

"I'd say we ought to take her," Gilroy said quietly.

For a split second Luddy felt his heart stop beating, then it made up for lost time. Gibby—Gilroy—Mr. McAfee had just saved an innocent child's future, and probably her life as well.

From around the room the men quickly gave their consent, now that their leader had spoken—all except Weldon and Bob. Continuing his role as the cool-headed logician, Thurston voiced concern that they must procure the required documents to take her out of the D.R. and into the United States. The group sent him and Luddy back to Repisa. There they would ask the mayor to draw up adoption papers.

"We'll have to take the baby with us," Thurston said. "They might want to ink her footprint on the certificate.

"Get back here with that van so we can start for the airport by sunup tomorrow," warned Sherm. "If you don't, Mendozo will be sure to come, knowing it's our flight date. Then he'll haul us off to jail, and it'll be ten years before we see the sunshine again."

"You talk like we're guilty," Keith Lawrence said. The collegian was already planning his appeal to the World Court in The Hague.

"It's not Sherm's talk, but Mendozo's I'm afraid of," said Thad. "His Spanish is so much more convincing."

There was nothing approaching an adoption form in the Repisa city hall, which was merely a room at the rear of the lumberyard office where Luddy had purchased metal roofing and was made an instant father.

"Thurston," Luddy said in an aside to his partner, "you're good at wording documents."

"I've created quite a few. Bid specifications, contracts and the like."

"Draw us up a contract. Put in all the *whereases* and *therefores* and the big words to make it legal. We'll put Felicité's footprint on it, get the mayor to sign it, and then we'll be in business."

Seated at his cluttered desk, which served both his public and private interests, the mayor approved of what was happening in his office. Thurston wrote at a small table, and Luddy walked back and forth burping the baby. Sr. Rodriguez admired Thurston's industry and Luddy's maternal instincts. He deemed the Americans' insistence on an official document commendable and, when Thurston had finished, liked what he drew up. He was impressed by the phrasing, especially favoring the *whereas* clauses as paragraphs of dignity. The mayor was known among the citizens of Repisa as a stickler for doing things properly. He himself was proud of his reputation.

"In fifteen years in this office," he said to his visitors, "no one yet has put anything over on me." He peppered his little speech with Spanish phrases, but Luddy thought he got the gist of his remarks.

Sr. Rodriguez stood, smiled, and chucked Felicité under the chin as they held her Lilliputian feet—first the right, then the left—to his ink pad and then printed the swirls of her satiny skin on the document. Nodding his head in support of the whole procedure, he carefully signed his name on the line next to Luddy's and Thurston's.

"Thank you, Mr. Mayor," Luddy said. He reached to take the paper from Rodriguez's desk. The mayor's hand, however, came down on his and with firmness removed it from the paper. Luddy looked up in surprise.

"Not yet," the mayor said. "The gold seal. Nothing is official without the gold seal."

"Oh, sure," said Luddy, relieved that holding up acquisition was nothing more than licking a gold seal and sticking it on a blank space next to the mayor's name.

Rodriguez opened a drawer of his desk, rifled through the contents, removed several papers, and searched thoroughly. Closing that drawer, he did the same for a second, then a third, and finally, the bottom drawer.

"No gold seals, huh?" asked Luddy, somewhere between disappointment and serious apprehension.

"I seem to have used my last seal," the mayor answered.

"This is good enough," Luddy said, again reaching for the document. "We don't mind if the paper lacks decoration."

"Non, non, señor. You do not understand." Rodriguez snatched up the paper and held it to his chest. "The officials in Santo Domingo will not like it without the decoration. All papers must have the gold seal."

When informed that they must hasten back to Santa María because on the following day they were to catch their plane in Santo Domingo, the mayor in genuine sympathy dispatched his teenage son to Constanza, a town some thirty miles away, to borrow a seal from that town's mayor.

"When will he get back?" Thurston asked.

"Tonight, late. Perhaps midnight."

There was nothing for Luddy, Thurston, and baby Felicité to do but to wait. Thankfully, the two men consoled themselves, the mayor possessed a fairly new Ford pickup, and the son, from what Luddy had heard on his visits to the lumberyard, was a fast driver.

"If he doesn't run off the road, he ought to be back in good time," Luddy said, trying to calm Thurston's butterflies. He did not mention what he had also heard—that the road to Constanza was paved, but had no straight stretch longer than fifty yards.

They ate their supper at a small outdoor cafe and returned twice to the restaurant to mix a bottle of formula for Felicité. By ten the town was lively with late diners crowding into three or four open courtyards where the tables were almost lost among the overflow of people. Lights strung from tree to tree and blaring music boosted the devil-may-care air that lifted the townspeople from their daily drudgery of field work to a few hours of relief bordering on ecstacy. For some tonight, nothing compared with the fun generated by two American *hombres* taking turns holding a very small baby, thrusting a bottle into its mouth, and occasionally extracting a diaper from a package of Pampers, using their table as a venue for changing.

The crowds surged through the streets, exchanging one restaurant for another and all the while getting noisier. The two Americans grew more silent. Seated at a table at the edge of the least boisterous establishment, they scanned the street over the rims of their Coke glasses for young Romero and his Ford. By one in the morning, the throngs began to wane, and so did prospects for Thurston and Luddy.

"*Señor* is here on business in our little town of Repisa?" asked a youth, dragging a chair to their table and sitting down.

"No," replied Luddy. "We're just a couple of . . . tourists."

"Oh, I thought you were businessmen," the youth said. He was in his late teens, his skin taut and tough, his hands hardened, and his manner exhibiting a touch of drunkenness. "You the business man, and he," nodding toward Thurston, "your driver. The *bebé*—?" He had no classification for the baby.

Luddy glanced at Thurston, then at himself, to determine why he would categorize them this way. The clothing—that was it. In packing for an early departure tomorrow, Luddy had rolled up his work clothes around the case of formula and at great effort succeeded in jamming the bulk into his carry-on flight bag. Besides, he had felt it might make their cause seem more important if he dressed in his suit while seeking the adoption papers. Thurston, of course, had no other clothes than the jeans and T-shirt he'd worn for the past three weeks and which, to this time, he had not been successful in retrading for his standard traveling outfit.

"In New York," the youth continued, "I saw American businessmen, they wore suits and neckties. I was in New York, you know, on a visit to my brother. In New York—"

Having been made conscious of his clothing, which ill-fitted this carefree scene, Luddy quite automatically straightened his tie and pulled down his jacket. In doing so, he felt something slightly bulging in the breast pocket of his coat. He pulled out two letters. One was from Meribel. The other from Magazine Reader's Sweepstakes. How had they got there? Oh, yes, now he remembered.

In his haste to leave the YMCA and get to the airport that morning they left home, he was handed two pieces of mail by the desk clerk. He'd pocketed them, intending to read them on the flight to Miami. But he'd forgotten, and not having worn his good clothes since arriving at Santa María, the letters had remained hidden from both view and memory these past three weeks.

He wanted to open Meribel's first, but felt the clamor around him was no setting for the tender words she'd undoubtedly had for him just before his trip. The other he would have dropped unopened into the wastebasket at home. But, here, to kill time, it was reading matter. He slit open the envelope and drew out several pieces of paper.

"This is it!" he exclaimed.

He jumped up, grabbing Thurston by the arm. "Bring Felicité! I've got the diapers. Back to the mayor's office! We'll get those adoption papers and be on our way!"

"If I can just get to New York again . . ." The young Dominican watched in bewilderment as the two men and their baby receded through the still rackety crowd and over the din heard their van start up.

He was in the midst of proposing a deal, hoping to persuade the Americans to enlist in his cause. But the Americans had vanished, and with them his chances of escaping the cane fields surrounding Repisa.

Chapter Fifteen

Since the van had no reverse gear, Luddy drove around the block, cutting corners short, and then to the limit of second gear, sped in the direction of the mayor's house next to the building-supply yard at the edge of town.

"He's probably gone to bed. I didn't see him in all that crowd," he said to Thurston, who held the baby tightly and figured she knew as much as he did about what was going on.

"What's up?" Thurston asked. "What was in that letter you opened—a bee or a rattlesnake—to get you to move so fast?"

"Better than that. Our ticket—Felicité's ticket—out of here."

He tossed the envelope to Thurston. Settling the baby on his knees, Thurston withdrew the contents.

"Sweepstakes. Junk mail."

"The gold seal. Find it?"

Close to the lights on the dashboard, Thurston examined the papers in his hand.

"See," explained Luddy, "it says, 'Remove the gold seal and affix to your entry blank'—or some such. Get it? Just what we've been waiting for all evening."

"We need a gold seal, but this one—"

"They'll never know the difference. Who reads what's on 'em?"

Thurston read, "Official Entry. Magazine Reader's Sweepstakes."

They pulled up in front of the mayor's house. In a few leaps, Luddy was at the door, Thurston and the baby right behind him. Luddy banged on the door. Nothing but darkness and silence. He banged again—steadily.

"*Ladrónes*. Thieves!" The cry bellowed from within.

"It's us, Sr. Rodriguez," shouted Luddy. "We've come for the *documento.*"

Bolts rattled and the door opened. The mayor, baring a weak flashlight, stood in the opening in his undershorts.

"Has Romero returned?" Luddy asked.

"Romero?" Rodriguez spoke the name as if he'd never once heard it.

"Your son."

"My son? *Sí, sí,* my son."

"He went to Constanza to borrow a gold seal."

"No, not come back. That boy, *pícaro*... he is a scoundrel. Probably stopped to carouse with his friends."

"No matter," said Luddy. "I've got the seal."

"Gold seal? You?"

"Yes, one came in a letter. All we need do is get Felicité's paper and stick it on."

"Paper?"

"*Documento*. The one we drew up this evening. Legalizing Felicité's adoption."

"*Documento* is in office." The mayor had been awakened bodily by Luddy's knock, though his brain was slow to stir. He retreated to the interior of the house and soon came back zipping up his trousers.

"Over here," he said, leading the way to his mayoral office.

In the light from a single bare bulb in the ceiling, Luddy gave a once-over to the clutter on the desk, and in a second or two focused on the only paper among a hundred that was of interest to him. Greedily, his eyes devoured it, and hardly diverting his gaze he peeled the seal from the sweepstakes flier and pressed it firmly to the adoption document.

"There!" he said, picking up the cherished paper.

"A moment," the mayor said, whisking it out of Luddy's hand, a motion at which he seemed adept.

"What now?"

"*Realzar*. I must emboss," replied the mayor. He opened a drawer in his desk and took out a small device, inserted the seal in its jaws and squeezed the handles together. The raised letters imprinted on the seal certified the document as an official act of the municipality of Repisa. On close scrutiny one might have assumed the town fathers had given their endorsement to participation in the chance giveaway of a million dollars.

"Now?" Luddy asked. Rodriguez nodded blankly.

"Thank you, Mr. Mayor." Clutching the paper, he started out the door, but turned back. From a pocket he extracted his plastic bag, which was down to a single jawbreaker. He thrust it toward the mayor.

"Help yourself," he said.

"Gracias."

Luddy turned again and raced to the van. With amazement, Thurston had watched Luddy's bamboozling with a phony decal, unable to say a word. Mesmerized, still without a word, he followed him to the van with the baby.

"Why do they send gold seal to you? You, a foreigner." From the doorway, Rodriguez called after them, shaping his words around the candy sphere in his mouth. Perhaps it was the sugar that stimulated the neurons in his brain. He was beginning to think more like the wise old man Luddy had judged him to be. "When has the post started coming at night?"

The van was already rolling. Luddy waved amiably but did not stop.

"Adiós!"

"Come back... you, you... *ladrón*... you... thief... you swindler! No one puts over anything on the mayor of Repisa!"

Never had the van sped so fast in a grinding second gear.

They arrived at Santa María hours after daybreak. Given the deplorable state of the road and the car's handicaps, Luddy attributed their getting there, if not to a miracle, at least to the Lord's direct intervention. He and Thurston had shared the driving and the feeding and diapering of Felicité. En route they discussed the higher right of a child's welfare over bureaucratic trivia and the means sometimes required to achieve it; the likelihood of Manuel Mendozo's return to Santa María to take his prisoners into custody, and their chances against unfair charges; the bleak outlook that Thurston would get his good clothes back because the village men had argued that a bargain was a bargain, and though they expressed gratitude and smiled broadly and said what they said politely, no amount of basic language or pantomime or hand signs on the part of the Americans was able to even chip their rock-hard stance.

As daylight brightened the trip, there came a lull in conversation, the baby slept peacefully, and thus far no one tailed them. This happy circumstance of having the road to themselves they no doubt owed to the probability that Romero was indeed what his father called him—a scoundrel. He was late in returning from Constanza, no doubt because he thought drinking with his friends was of greater priority, or at least more satisfying, than delivering to waiting foreigners some old circular scrap of paper coated with gold paint. With these conditions prevailing, Luddy felt the time was right for settling back and enjoying Meribel's letter. Once into it, however, he neither felt settled nor found the reading enjoyable. The letter was utterly blunt.

For several weeks I've believed we should deter-

mine the direction our relationship is going in.

With this, he was in full agreement. It was the next sentence that bothered him.

If you're serious, I will expect some word to that effect from you while you are on this trip. We've been seeing each other at least twice or three times a week for almost fifteen years, more or less. Now that we're separated for three weeks, you should have the opportunity for some objective thinking. You should know how I feel just by my raising the issue and asking for your response. Phone or cable or write me—at least send a postcard, and give me a hint as to what you're thinking.

With nothing but silence from him, what was she to think? When he got home, maybe he could borrow the use of his sister's fireplace. The misconception Meribel was sure to harbor called for no less than setting it right face-to-face. No plane could fly him home fast enough.

"From Meribel?" asked Thurston. "How'd you manage to get a letter from home?"

"Hand-delivered."

"What d'ya mean?"

"She left it at the Y before we started the trip."

"Oh, I see. One of those kind you read over and over, is that it?"

"I wish I could say I've read it every day for the past three weeks. The truth is, I just now opened it and read it for the first time."

"You waited this long?" Thurston shook his head in admiration. "What discipline!"

The men who had remained in Santa María were ready to quit the village the instant the van stopped in front of the church. They climbed in, having no luggage to stow, not even the tools they had brought to the village. These they had offered in exchange for their suits and shirts and ties, but failed to persuade the village men to give up their new badges of respectability. Resigned to flying back to the States in T-shirts and jeans, cut-offs, and too-short shorts, first one then another among the Americans, last of all Gilroy McAfee, said, "What the . . . Might as well leave 'em our tools, too."

Luddy was ready for departure; Felicité, her bottles and diapers, his bag, all were aboard, so nothing but the farewells kept them from going. "We've already said good-bye," Harry informed him. "So let's go before Mendozo comes with other plans."

Almost as many villagers were present to see them off as had been drawn through curiosity at their coming three weeks earlier. Bernabé had planned a little farewell ceremony to express the people's gratitude for the school, but this had to be summed up in one parting shot caught by the Americans as Weldon lurched them in second gear toward the winding path up to the mountain ridge: "*Gracias, señores!* God bless!"

In the sight of the villagers, the van shrank in size as it advanced up the mountain road. For a long while they watched it, waving all the time. Several asked their leader why the government would want to hold as prisoners these men who without ever being asked had done them such a great kindness. How surprised *Padre* would be when he returned. For years, they'd begged the government for a school, but always there was no money. Now they had three rooms, benches on which the children would sit, and money to buy books and paper and pencils and a blackboard for the teacher to write on. Why did the Americans descend on their tiny village one day, as if from heaven itself, and the next day each man pitch in as if he were building a house for his own private use?

Their question stumped Bernabé. Like others, he was glad their celestial friends had escaped the power of the man in the gold-encrusted uniform. If it was demanded of him as their jailer, he would say they were able to flee because the villagers had no weapons with which to keep them. It probably would not put the Americans in the light they deserved, but as a bald statement it would be true.

"We could not keep them even for the farewell we'd planned," Bernabé said to his people.

"The *Americanos,*" said one who had worked with them every day, "they wished to keep us from saying thanks, so they hurried away. They wanted no credit."

"No credit," added a second workman. "They did it for God."

The van inched up the zigzag route toward the ridge, straining and chugging, and trailing a small cloud of blue smoke. Common sense said the men depending on this crippled conveyance should have worried whether it would take them all the way to the airport at Santo Domingo. But the experiences of the last three weeks had given them more to think about than stripped gears and overburdened engines. Their stay in the valley had been a veritable college course combining geography, cultural anthropology, and international relations. If they hadn't feared that Mendozo would at any moment swoop down and cart them off to prison, they would have been reluctant to leave. Each had his favorite family, his preferred workman, his special memory of life in the village.

On their last night there, a lustrous moon had washed the stark streets of Santa María, and to Sherm Boyer and Thad Johnson this tiny, quiet spot was the most peaceful scene on earth. They had stepped through the window of their officially secured quarters so as not to compromise their dutiful guards outside the door, and for most of an hour strolled among the homes, saying good-bye to those who had become their friends over the past three weeks. Three times they had come to the plaza in front of the church. Reaching it a fourth time and finding the church door open, they paused before it, looking in. Candles burned before the altar and at a small shrine halfway down the right aisle. Their flames picked out garlands of wild flowers circling images of María and her Son.

"Different from back home, huh?" Sherm whispered to Thad.

"Please enter," said a voice approaching from behind them. One of the men who had worked faithfully on the school took Thad by the arm and practically pulled him inside. "It's all right. You come visit our church."

"Thanks," Sherm said for Thad and himself. "You go do what you came for. We'll just stand in the back here for a few minutes."

The man walked forward, kneeling and crossing himself frequently. Near the altar a teenage girl and an old woman prayed.

"Yeah, it's different all right," Thad said, and he seated himself on a crude bench.

Though Santa María's church was small and possessed none of the rich treasures of larger, more important temples, it brought Rosewood Church to the men's minds as plain, even bare. "I suppose there're greater differences than just in the building," said Sherm. But how were he and Thad or any of them to know what differences? They knew what Rosewood believed: the fundamentals of the faith, that the Word of God was sure, that salvation was the gift of heaven, that Christ was the key. They naturally would expect differences with a Catholic church. And neither did they exactly believe every jot and tittle of Presbyterian or Methodist doctrine—at least that of some Presbyterians, Methodists, and Baptists—and maybe who else. Yet, over these past weeks they and the people of Santa María had seemed to share a common bond.

Whenever passages were read from Luddy's Bible and the words were put into the villager's language, the people reacted as if they were the owners of the parable of the Prodigal or the story of Calvary. As Sherm thought about it, the Word became the great test—accept it or reject it. Plenty of churches in the United States had turned from it or trivialized it. These people did not.

The two Americans left the church knowing little more about it than when they went in, but as they made their way to the window to re-enter what they jokingly called the hoosegow, they sensed their visit to this small dot of civilization had been worthwhile.

"For what God is doing in us—as much as what he might do in them," Sherm said, half to himself, and Thad, struggling to pass his corpulency headfirst over the sill, asked what Sherm had said, but received no answer.

"I'm glad we landed in the wrong Santa María," said Thad as the van labored up the mountain road. He said it without conjuring up the grim consequences he usually saw at the end of every avenue open to them.

"A school for Santa María of the Snow this year, a school for *del Sud* next year," proposed Luddy, who fed Felicité her bottle.

"Does that mean a girl this year, and a boy next?" cracked Bob Franklin.

"Hey, Luddy" called Sherm Boyer, who as they neared the top had turned for one last look into the valley. "That mayor of the town you went to, did you guys say he might chase you because of that flake of a gold seal?"

"It wasn't a flake," objected Thurston. "As much gold on it as you can expect on any gold seal."

"Well, never mind the karats. Somebody's started up the trail behind us."

Each man craned his neck to look. They could just make out a vehicle leaving Santa María. "Sure enough," said Luddy. "I'd say it's a pickup truck, all right. No doubt the mayor's."

"Romero must have finally got home from Constanza," said Thurston, "and now the old man is hot to take back Felicité's paper. Can't you step on it a bit more, Weldon?"

"This jalopy ain't goin' nowhere," Weldon said, remembering to engage the clutch as he applied the brakes. "There's a bus up ahead and no place for either him or us to pass or turn out."

What Weldon said was true. The road narrowed to two tracks in this stretch at the top and for a hundred yards or so was bordered by dangerously steep slopes on either side.

"Mendozo!" cried Bob, and the others echoed his alarming deduction. The small bus coming toward them, once a school bus in the States, had to be the customs officer's promised paddy wagon.

In front, an arm of the law whose only aim was to throw them in prison for what they didn't do; behind, an angry village potentate who accounted himself deceived by men he had trusted. And on each side, a drop of a hundred feet or more. Truly, the Americans were the center attraction.

"With that bus blocking the way, we can't go forward," Weldon said. "And we couldn't back up if we wanted to. Not in this crate."

The bus halted less than a yard from the van's front bumper.

"Ludlow," called Gilroy from the rear seat of the van. "You're the only free man among us. Maybe you should be the one to talk with

Sr. Mendozo."

Luddy passed the baby to his nearest seat companion, Keith Lawrence, and the college student, who had a fear of females under the age of eighteen, immediately handed her off to his quiet, receptive neighbor, Steve Hatfield.

Luddy jumped out of his seat and onto the scant footing alongside. Perhaps adding to the qualifications McAfee gave him were his clothes. Contrasted with theirs, his was formal attire and made him the only member of their group that a fastidious official like the gilded Mendozo would feel comfortable dealing with. At this point, Luddy thought it better if Mendozo was made to feel very comfortable.

The customs officer stepped down from the bus and gingerly picking his way beside it, reached the tiny no-man's land where the vehicles met. He accosted Luddy.

"Where do you men think you are going? Did I not put you all under arrest?"

"Not me," Luddy said.

"Hmmmm. No, not you, *señor*. But the others. They were to remain under guard until I returned with a bus."

That was said to Luddy's perfect understanding. In fact, whatever Mendozo said was easily understood. Luddy guessed he had learned English in New Haven or perhaps Buffalo. But now was not the time to speculate on the man's academic background. The freedom of his friends depended on this encounter with one who unquestionably possessed the upper hand. But always in the crunch, Luddy had been tongue-tied. He'd always failed to speak when his speaking would have made a difference. Put to the test once again, he'd try.

"The people of Santa María faithfully guarded your prisoners," he said as a beginning. "Every night two men sat watch at the door. But you gave them no weapons, so you didn't really expect them to prevent the Americans from going on holiday, did you?"

"Holiday?"

"We wondered if you'd ever really come back. Maybe you were too busy for such an insignificant case as ours. So, presuming you had more important things to do, we thought a little drive in the mountains . . ." He was gaining confidence.

"Hmmm. You were planning to circle around and end your holiday back at the village, were you not?"

"Well, no. More like the airport at Santo Domingo."

"But that's impossible. These men are under arrest."

"True. But for what purpose?" He felt emboldened now. He pressed their case. "What is their crime?"

"Smuggling drugs into the country." Like a hounding lawyer, Mendozo took a step closer to Luddy. He did not want this American to miss the triumph spreading over his face.

"Just what drugs did they smuggle into your country?" Luddy asked.

"Heroin. Or maybe cocaine. Something. We found a white substance in the Termos they had in their room."

"Probably talc."

"Talk?"

"Talc." Luddy patted his face and mimed the sprinkling of powder in his armpits, and in doing so threw his shoulder out of joint. Resorting to the usual remedy, he frightened Mendozo, who mistook the windmill windup as coiling for a knockout blow. Mendozo jumped back, lost his footing and heaved head over heels down the steep slope, screaming in two languages.

The driver of the bus sprang to the door and from the safety of the bottom step leaned out and looked down. Luddy's companions skittered from the van, all sure that justice had sent their jailer plunging to his grave. They crowded to the front of the vehicles, hanging on to wheel wells and outside mirrors lest a misstep should send them to join him somewhere down below. Only Luddy remained calm. Planting one foot firmly in the road and the other digging into the slope, he stretched his arm down—not the one that had caused the problem.

"Grab hold, Sr. Mendozo," he called, sincere in the invitation. The customs officer lay wrapped around a shrub, the only growth in a large expanse around. The scrubby bush stood about six feet below the road.

"Are you a murderer, too?" spluttered Mendozo, who with Luddy's help was once again on his feet. Injured most seriously was his dignity. He was covered with dirt, his trousers were torn. The gold braid on his jacket was definitely tarnished. His cap had rolled far into the ravine.

"You oughta be careful, sir," Luddy admonished. "It's a terrible long way to the bottom." He brushed at the poor fellow's clothes, but Mendozo wanted no help. His best recovery was to pretend that no one had seen him duck from what appeared to be a physical attack in the making, or that none had heard his inelegant screams, and that all eyes had not gaped as he lay helplessly horizontal. He was mortified that at a crucial point in his mission—a mission he had initiated and insisted he could carry out with no assistance—he had sullied his uniform and thereby had dishonored the service it represented. How was he to regain command over his American prisoners? They must be laughing at his predicament. He could bluster and come down hard on the men. But they'd laugh inwardly. He could send them back to the village with a reprimand, and himself go back to Santo Domingo and write an official close to the case. Given time, he could think his way out of this embarrassment, probably with a measure somewhere in between. But this brash young man whose convolutions had sent him flying wasn't about to allow him time.

"Sorry I scared you," apologized Luddy.

Scared? In English, that meant frightened. His position did not allow him to admit fright.

"Nothing you did," he said, hoping to hide his first outburst. "The ground merely gave way." To illustrate, Mendozo dug in the earth with his foot and sent a tiny avalanche over the side.

"Glad you're okay," said Luddy. "It'd take a long time for me to forget I'd scared a fine, upstanding customs officer to his grave."

"You did *not* frighten me," insisted Mendozo. Having only felt and not seen the abrasions on his cheek and chin that blood and dirt had caked with mud, he sucked in his stomach, pushed back his shoulders, and strove for an air of formality.

"The charge," he said, as if nothing had caused an interruption, "is smuggling drugs into the Dominican Republic."

"Well, explain to me, Sr. Mendozo, at what point a person legally enters your country. When the plane lands or when the passenger's foot touches the ground?"

When a man's foot hurtles over the precipice? Mendozo steeled himself to cast personal troubles behind him and to stick to his department's business.

"When a foreigner passes through customs and the immigration agents," he said. "At that point he has legally entered."

"And that's when smuggling, if smuggling's going to be done, occurs?"

What was this fellow driving at? It was hard to think straight when still before him flashed that steep, steep slope down which he had tumbled faster than he had ever moved in all his life. He was further diverted by someone handing him his cap.

"I think this is yours?" Sherm Boyer bobbed his head in deference to the officer.

"Why, yes. You . . . went all the way to the bottom to rescue my cap?"

"Not as fast as you started down," Sherm said with a little laugh.

"Thank you. That was thoughtful. I would have left it there, though it means much to me."

"Smuggling occurs when something gets through customs, right?" Luddy had a point to make, and remembering the pickup headed toward them he was not sure how long he had to make it in.

"Slipping through immigration and customs," Mendozo said, glad to get back to business.

"Okay. That being the case, you'll recall that my friends here all passed through customs and immigration."

"Yes, of course. The next day after their arrival."

"And what did they carry through with them?"

"You had a bag and there was a stack of building instruments."

"Which all passed the scrutiny of your eagle-eyed men."

"All was approved."

"And what else did the men carry with them?"

"Nothing. Remarkably nothing, their luggage having gone on to Bolivia."

"Nothing carried in. No Thermos. It was left behind, forgotten."

"Hmmmm. Yes. We found it later."

"So if the narcotics on which you base your case against my friends did not enter your country, no crime was committed. Do you agree, Sr. Mendozo?"

"Agree? Hmmmm. There's the Termos."

"Which may have contained talc."

At the mention of the word, Mendozo nearly panicked. He

grasped a fender of the bus to avoid a repeat of what he believed was that word's vendetta against him.

"But if no narcotics or even talcum powder entered through customs, there was no crime. Right?"

"Why, no, I suppose not." He was beginning to see a way to quickly end this humiliating encounter.

"So on what grounds are these men under arrest?"

"Well . . . I put them under arrest." He could not relinquish all authority. "That is all the grounds needed."

"But they will have a trial?"

"Of course, ours is a democratic country."

"And when Sr. Mendozo, who, I'm sure, has an unblemished record for convictions against offending foreigners, brings his charges in court, what will you say?"

What would he say? Maybe when the time came, he'd think of something to say. Now, he could think of nothing. He only wanted to get out of this place.

"Well . . . I will let the men go—this time."

"Thank you, sir, and I believe I speak for all of them, too."

The accused gave a cheer, including in the homage both Luddy's name and Mendozo's. The commotion had not died when Harry punctured the good feeling.

"Your angry mayor is gaining on us, Luddy. Better do something, quick."

"Ask this guy in the gold braid to keep the mayor from taking away our baby," Weldon said. Luddy noted the "our baby". "I'm sure he can help."

"Sr. Mendozo," Luddy said. The customs officer had turned back to the bus.

"Yes?"

"I know you're on the way down into the valley to release the villagers from your order to hold the Americans prisoner. Besides it being part of your official duty, I know you, as an honest man, would complete your task."

"Of course," Mendozo said drily.

"But you can't go forward, and neither can we because there is no room for either vehicle to pass. So, if we traded our van for your bus, we could both reach our destination."

"But this bus is a governmental vehicle."

"And ours is owned by a distinguished worldwide empire."

"You want to trade?"

"Temporarily. Hertz will want its van back as much as the Dominican Republic will want its bus."

"And where would the second exchange take place?"

"At the airport. As close to the departure gate as possible."

"Hmmm. I suppose we can do that. But Sr. Ruddy—it is Sr. Ruddy, is it not?—we must not enter this transaction into the official records—"

"Of course not. Only us and you and your driver—"

"He's under my orders. And one thing more. You won't report our little misunderstanding about the Termos, or about our meeting here, to your embassy or the newspapers?"

"Never in a thousand years." Weldon passed the van keys to Luddy, and he handed them over to Mendozo.

"One thing about the van," Luddy said as the van contingent boarded the bus and Mendozo climbed into the van. "In backing down the hill, don't start the engine. Just push the clutch in and keep one foot on the brake."

The Rosewood men were happy to leave the driving to the driver, who asked no questions but understood the word airport. They quickly stowed Luddy's bag and settled back, Luddy mothering the baby once more. Slowly, the bus started in reverse. Before Mendozo could ease the van back down toward the village, the Ford pickup, with the mayor behind the wheel and his son seated alongside, pulled to the top of the ridge, stopping just short of the van. Rodriguez jumped out and ran screeching toward the retreating bus.

"Stop them. Stop . . . *ladrónes* . . . thieves . . . scoundrels!"

Mendozo was not interested in prolonging his meeting with the Americans on this mountain, or of starting one with a wild, screaming native of these parts—even one accorded the title of mayor, so he sat unmoving in the van. The bus picked up speed, with its ten American passengers, all of them freed men, and a baby whose status was somewhat doubtful. It soon rolled beyond the mayor's reach and in a couple of minutes was completely out of his voice range.

Chapter Sixteen

"Trouble at *Pasaporte!* Trouble at *Pasaporte!*" The voice bawled urgently in Spanish over the public address system. The Americans might not have understood the message had they not been in the midst of the trouble, or to put it more accurately, been the cause of it.

The Rosewood men, looking like impoverished *campesinos,* had inched forward in two lines to have their passports stamped and then to move into the airport departure lounge to await their flight to the United States. The last of the group in his line, Luddy carried the tightly blanketed Felicité in one arm. In his free hand he held his passport and the baby's adoption paper. He wasn't sure these two documents fulfilled all the technicalities of international travel, but hoped for sympathetic handling by the man up ahead in the immigration window.

His turn came to be checked out of the country. Dutifully he laid his passport on the counter, and with more cunning than comfortably fit him, waved the paper enough to gain it attention but not scrutiny, his thumb covering all but the edges of the questionable gold seal. The agent had time only to ask, "Traveling with a child, Mr. Newton?" when a commotion broke out in the adjacent line. Bob Franklin had challenged Weldon Basker as to who should be processed first, and Weldon was not one to let a challenge pass unchallenged.

"*Motín*, riot," yelled the officer whose line's decorum was desecrated by the ugly Americans. Luddy's man looked up at his neighboring officer, nervously hoping the trouble would not spread to his domain.

"Call headquarters," pleaded the victimized agent. He darted from his cage, intent on separating the two who were pushing and slapping each other.

Fortunately for the belligerents, and for the agents as well, Sr. Mendozo was not present today. The chief hated any disruption to the smooth flow of people and goods at the airport. Talk among the agents this morning was that their boss had gone to the country to round up some dangerous foreigners.

With his attention riveted on the two shouting, shoving Americans, and quite absent from his duties, Luddy's agent picked up his phone with one hand and with the other quickly stamped the passport before him and impatiently waved its owner on past the barrier. It would be some time before Luddy and the others of their group learned what happened next, for when Luddy and Felicité passed into the departure lounge they entered another world, one that was calm to the point of boring and immune to diplomatic particulars.

Out in the larger hall, before the distress call could be broadcast, Weldon and Bob halted their brawl, as suddenly as they had started it, shook hands, clasped each other around the neck, and in great politeness deferred one to the other, each insisting he be the last to be processed for the flight home. Their purpose had been achieved—the baby was safely inside, now forgotten by the land of its birth. In two minutes they would join their friends in the lounge, and within half an hour they should be airborne.

They had not, however, reckoned with Manuel Mendozo. Just back from his exasperating and rather purposeless trip to Santa María la Real de Nieva, and in more disarray than his staff had ever witnessed, he was hastening to his office when he heard the call on the terminal's public address system. Diverting to the scene of the problem, he arrived at the same time that a squad of police converged on the passport area.

"Trouble?" He demanded of his agents. "What trouble?"

"These two *Americanos* were fighting," one of the officers explained. "But it's over now. Everything is all right."

Mendozo took one quick look at Weldon Basker and Bob Franklin and, forgetting for the moment that a dusty uniform and a lacerated face tarnished if not his authority, his dignity, said, "Everything's not all right. It's not over. Lock these two hoodlums in the detention room. And if any more of their friends come through, lock them up, too."

But no more Americans awaited a passport check. They were

already in the sanitized zone just minutes from stepping aboard a plane for Miami. Weldon and Bob alone were dispatched to the makeshift prison. They had one consolation: three weeks before ten men had been squeezed into the room; today there was ample space for each of the recidivists to stretch out. Considering Mendozo's mood toward certain American travelers, they possibly could be in for a long rest.

In a few minutes the flight was called. Wondering what had happened to their two companions, the Rosewood men left the lounge as directed and walked over the tarmac to the plane. Appreciating the ruse that made easy passage for the baby, they nonetheless reasoned that Weldon and Bob were big boys now and with three weeks of varied training should be able to take care of themselves. Outside, their attention was captured by someone shouting the name of their leader.

"Mr. McAfee. Mr. Gilroy McAfee."

Looking back and above the lounge exit, they saw a tall, swart figure lean over the rail of an observation deck. He wore jeans and a pale blue T-shirt, and a baseball cap shaded his eyes. This was not their image of a pastor, but they instinctively knew he was the man they had somehow missed.

"That guy's calling you, Gibby."

"I am Gilroy McAfee. Who wants me?"

"I am Juan Cristóbal. Pastor Juan of Santa María del Sud."

"Where have you been?" Sherm Boyer asked sharply. "You're about three weeks late."

"I was here the day you said you arrive. But no one came out that door from customs. I asked if any *Americanos* inside. A fellow looked and saw none."

"We were kept in a—" Harry was cut off by Gilroy.

"I thought, 'Maybe, Juan, you got wrong month,'" Juan went on. "'Probably they come February, not January.' So I go north on my preaching mission."

"We were held pris—"

"Never mind." Gilroy hushed Harry's intended confession. "He wouldn't understand."

"So how come you're here today?" Harry asked, taking a new tack.

"If January *was* right month, today is your day to leave Dominican Republic. I here to see if you really came."

Gilroy teetered anxiously as the last of the passengers, other than themselves, disappeared into the plane. Wishing to wrap it up, he said, "We did build a school—in another Santa María."

"My people still waiting."

"Next year," offered Luddy.

The Americans then scrambled up the steps.

Though Felicité's adoption was done in Luddy's name, it would soon be known around Rosewood Church that she was a child of the congregation. A novel arrangement, yes, but one intriguing to many of the members. Thurston and Amy Biddle were the first to have her, to be followed by the Steve Hatfields, the Thad Johnsons, the Sherm

Boyers and, their criminal records notwithstanding, Weldon Basker and Bob Franklin, and their wives.

Weldon and Bob arrived home two days after the others. For forty-eight hours Luís, now an old friend as well as jailer, attended to their basic needs. Besides each other, he was the only person they encountered. They had ample time not only to speculate on a dubious future but to come to terms with the troublesome and acrimonious year just passed. Perhaps it was sharing the scare of three arrests in three weeks and having no one to seat except each other that turned these rival ushers into brothers under the skin. When they both acknowledged that this current sacrifice of their freedom was worth an innocent baby's future, they discovered there was more to unite them than to pit them as competitors and foes.

On the third morning of their captivity, Luís pulled back the deadbolt that barred their door. Manuel Mendozo in a new spangled uniform, stood before them.

"You have just time to board your plane to the States," he said, and led them as willing followers to it. In the two days since locking them up, he had vacillated over his pesky quarry. In the end, he decided his days would improve if the last of these Americans were gone completely out of his life. He personally stamped their passports and pushed them into the departure lounge.

"*Adiós,* Sr. Mendozo," Weldon said, waving his hand gratefully.

"See you next year," Bob added. Before Mendozo could accurately translate into his native tongue what he had just heard and his mind could digest it, Bob whisked his partner through the doorway to freedom.

Luddy missed the daily care of the baby, though he acknowledged it would be rather difficult to tend her while driving the recycling truck. A deep concern rode the truck with him, however, the more immediate problem born of his relationship with Meribel.

Unlike some forty members of the church, Meribel did not go to the airport to welcome the school builders. She did not see the baby that astounded the welcoming committee—an eleventh member of the team who caused more fomentation even than the scraggly beards that covered once-familiar faces, and the wild array of tattered shirts and ill-fitting pants that were in such contrast to the Sunday suits in which the men had left home a scant three weeks earlier. Not knowing that Luddy had turned the baby over to Thurston and Amy as her first parents—or even that there was a baby—or anything that went on at the men's homecoming, except that they were back, with Luddy among them, she answered the door with nearly a blank sheet of paper inserted in her mind when that evening he rang her bell. Nearly blank. One notation was on it. Standing in the doorway, eyeing this one who had been completely out of her life for three weeks, apparently by his own choosing, she was not certain she wanted to let him in.

"Gosh, it's great to see ya, Meribel." Luddy's smile was as broad as his face; a tuft of hair stood up board-straight, as if a flag of friendship. It was enough to dent her outward armor. She invited him to come in and sit down. With forethought, he picked the sofa. She sat in a chair across the room.

"It's been three weeks—" He hardly knew how to begin.

"Oh, you kept track of time?" She resolved to be difficult. He had ignored her appeal for some communication. Now it was her turn to show indifference.

"You bet we did. The first week went kinda slow. We had to find the materials to build with, and the foundation and floor took longer than expected. Then the second week things moved into high gear. That's when Felicité came."

"Felicité?"

"Yeah. Some baby she is! We brought her with us. You'll love her."

"You brought . . . some babe . . . home with you?"

"Sure thing. It took some doing, but we did."

It had taken some doing all right. While his companions were returning the bus at the airport, Luddy spoke with a member of the American consulate. The immigration authorization that others labored sometimes for months to obtain he got in twenty minutes. But that was Luddy. Of this he said nothing to Meribel. He thought she'd be more interested in the short-running drama at *Pasaporte*.

"Weldon and Bob staged a little sideshow that helped me get her through passport check. I guess they're still in jail."

"In jail? Who's in jail? Because you got this babe—"

"Weldon and Bob. They faked a fight so in the commotion I could slip her into the departure lounge."

Meribel sniffed. "*You* slipped her in?"

"Yeah. They all sort of looked on her as my girl. But they all took turns with her."

Meribel couldn't believe what she was hearing. Once she'd been dumbfounded that Luddy had looked at a couple of girlie magazines, but he'd convinced her his curiosity was purely cerebral. Now she didn't know. He wasn't talking just about pictures. "You certainly don't mean Gilroy McAfee 'had his turn,' as you say."

"Oh, Gibby—the guys call him Gibby now—he was real sweet around Felicité. You should have seen him give her a bath!"

"Oh!" She shaded her eyes. "Don't tell me any more. To think you men representing a perfectly respectable church went down to the Caribbean and came back with a girl you took turns with, and gave baths to, and who *you* slipped past the authorities!"

"Oh, it was all legal, except maybe the gold seal. But putting that over paled to the satisfaction of bringing Felicité with us."

Puzzled by her shock, he thought he had better go back to the beginning.

"We would have written, but where we were, the village was kinda isolated. I never saw a mail carrier or even a recycling truck in the whole three weeks."

"Is that why I received no answer to my letter?"

"Well—" He lowered his head and with his shoe tip traced the design in Meribel's carpet. "To tell you the truth, the three weeks was nearly up before I opened your letter."

"Three weeks! Is that all a letter of mine means to you? Were you so taken up with this . . . this Felicité that a letter from me was so much junk mail that you threw it on a pile to be opened later?"

"I forgot I had it. I honestly did. I picked it up before leaving the Y that morning and stuck it in the pocket inside my jacket. That and a sweepstakes entry form."

"I hope you did better with the sweepstakes."

"Oh, I did. It was a lifesaver. I don't mean I won a million dollars, but the gold seal that came with it, we used it in place of the real thing, and it turned out good enough to get Felicité out of the country."

She wanted to cry, but resolutely erected a very firm dam that held back the tears that the break in a long relationship was bound to bring. She stood up, a signal that he should go.

"My department at the store is remodeling tomorrow," she said, quite as a matter-of-fact. "I'll do better if I get some sleep."

When last they'd met, Luddy had pecked her on the cheek. Racing to her house this evening, he had hoped they'd quickly settle the neglected letter so the kiss he'd give her would be long and passionate. Instead, in great disappointment, he merely said, "I don't suppose you want a jawbreaker? No? Well, 'Bye. See ya 'round."

Friday was now the regular recycling day for Travis Street. Approaching the 900 block, Luddy looked down and midway saw Beulah Simms at the curb, next to her yellow container. As he drew closer, he saw she was holding a Thermos jug and three mugs. He smiled and said to Carlos and Jake, his jumpers, "I hope this Thermos doesn't get people into trouble like the last one I saw."

Neither man understood, and as he stopped the truck in front of Mrs. Simms' house, Luddy said to never mind. She held out the mugs.

"Welcome home," she called. "I knew you'd be along. Your replacement could never make it on time. I got some fresh cider yesterday. I thought you'd like it hot."

The crew paused long enough for the refreshment, then at Luddy's word forged ahead. He appreciated these acts of kindness on the part of Mrs. Simms, but nothing rivaled the collecting of recyclable materials; he was glad that nothing foreseeable would keep him away from the task until next year when they went to the Dominican Republic again.

"Hey, Carlos," he said. The jumpers rode in the cab as they turned the corner and cut over to Holcomb for the reverse direction. "How about teaching Spanish to me and my friends?"

"I no teacher," Carlos said, grinning at the thought of standing between a blackboard and a room full of desks, as he had seen on PTA night at his kids' school.

"Not a regular teacher," Luddy added. "You just talk, then we'll ask you what you said."

"Maybe."

"And we'll pay you."

"*Sí. Sí.* Why not I teach?"

"We'll start in the spring, and then by next winter when we go back to the D.R. the whole gang'll be speaking like the natives."

Luddy discovered that Meribel wasn't so willing to talk, though. All Friday evening he tried to phone her, but there was no answer. He was disappointed when he finally did get her. She admitted she'd heard the ring but ignored it. There would be no visit to the library on Saturday night. And he was not to come around to pick her up on Sunday. She had a headache and was sure it would not let up in time for church.

Once again Luddy was down on himself for striking out. How could he forget to read her letter? Before leaving Miami for Santo Domingo, he should have called her and said yes, he was serious, yes, he saw marriage in their future. During those three weeks of silence, she naturally believed he had rejected her plea to think deeply about commitment, that he was too uncertain to commit himself to a joint future with her. But he *had* forgotten, and with his confession, she apparently thought it even worse for him to forget—out of sight, she was out of his mind.

Over the weekend he did not try again to contact her. Monday night he talked to the desk clerk at the Y for a couple of hours. He related the good times he and his friends had had in the D.R., saying they could even look back on their incarcerations and laugh. He thought it funny that those who had grown beards removed them within a day or two after returning home.

"Serves 'em right for bein' married," the clerk said. Luddy refrained from talking about Felicité and Meribel.

He went to his room and thought about them. An hour later the night clerk trudged up to the third floor to call him to the phone.

"Can't you get your girlfriend to call you before midnight?" the clerk complained.

"Girlfriend? You mean Meribel's on the line?"

"How should I know? Some gal who said to get you even if I had to drag you outta bed."

Luddy did not need to be dragged. He ran down the stairs, three steps at a time.

It was Meribel, all right.

"Oh, Luddy, I've been so wrong," she began, a bit weepy.

"Well, it was my fault—forgetting your letter."

"No, not about that. About Felicité."

"I didn't know she was a problem."

"With me she was. My biggest problem. When you said you brought home a baby I thought you meant... a... *baby*... a... a... you know... a *babe*. I thought of a young girl, maybe a teenager . . . one of those Latin . . . floozies."

"Meribel!" It was Luddy's turn to express horror.

"I know. I just found out you meant a baby... a baby."

"Yeah. That's what I said—a baby."

"Oh, Luddy, I'm so sorry. Can you ever forgive me?"

"Sure. I'm not mad."

Before he reported for work Tuesday morning, Luddy went around to see Meribel. Again, she apologized. She forgave him for forgetting to read her letter. She said that what she wrote then, she still meant. She was ready to commit. Luddy said nothing and stared hard at the floor.

"If you're thinking of my little pique over Mrs. Simms' attention to you before you and the men left for your mission, I'm over that," she said. "I've come to realize that Beulah Simms thinks she's got to mother you, and that maybe you can stand a little mothering—by one old enough to be your mother, or grandmother."

Luddy said, yeah, she was probably right. But now he had to think about picking up aluminum cans and old newspapers. He really did have to be on his way.

" 'Bye," he said, displaying a grin that was only half his usual output.

They went to prayer meeting together Wednesday night, and to the library on Saturday, and on the way home he suggested that they stop by Thurston and Amy Biddle's so she could meet Felicité.

"Oh, I don't think we should," Meribel said. "We'd probably wake her up, and I don't know what to do when a baby cries."

He went around to pick her up for church on Sunday morning. On the way, they talked about many things and laughed at some of them. On the way home, they had lunch at Denny's and confined their talk to two topics, both of which had originated at church and would master the conversation of every church family's dinner table.

From the pulpit, the Reverend Peter Barrett had announced his resignation and acceptance of a call to Topeka, Kansas. And next month, Gilroy and Bessie McAfee were moving to Florida.

Chapter Seventeen

Never in his life had Gilroy McAfee had so good a time as his three weeks in the Dominican Republic. The chairman of the Deacon Board hammered and sawed consistently in building the school for Santa María, which at day's end left him a tired old man, but with a feeling of accomplishment. He mingled freely with the villagers; at one time or another he'd pop his head in at a doorway to exchange a friendly greeting, and frequently would accept an invitation to share a family's meal. He developed enough skill at sign language to understand and be understood. He enjoyed the company of the fellows on the mission, laughed with them, entered into serious discussions, admitted his foibles, and was one who had grown a beard—perhaps out of convenience, or maybe even out of mild cultural rebellion. He readily had bowed to the nickname that a bumbling customs official had given him, and which the team members had taken up—Gibby.

But Gilroy was home now. He was once again properly attired and clean-shaven. He could no longer afford to be Gibby. At the church, he had communion plates to pass, solemn board meetings to conduct; at home, he had a wife to nurse through her real and imaginary wounds to both body and spirit.

Try as he might, it was hopeless he'd shed his nickname and regain his once differentiated standing among the men he had led on the Caribbean mission. And to make up for the time her husband was gone, Bessie complained more every day that the injuries she suffered at the hands of exuberant twelve-year-old boys would get no better as long as those boys were around the church and she had to live in fear that the lightning of their overzealous activity could strike a second time.

The implication in "Gibby" and the decomposing discipline of the deacons and Bessie herself, some said, combined to cause McAfee to sell the house, pack the car, and head permanently for new surroundings in Florida.

It probably didn't help settle his spirit that in the first board meeting after the mission the deacons chose as the new pew Bibles Luddy's modern version that had been their only copy of the Scriptures at Santa María. It wasn't that Gilroy was opposed to the clearer, more up-to-date language, since during those three weeks he had looked forward to each morning's reading of a chapter or two in words all easily understood. But reading "you" in reference to God was one thing in the barracks-like quarters of men in casual mode; it was another to think that "thee" and "thou" would never be heard in church again, except when now and then the pastor through lapse of memory slipped one in while praying. Before the vote on the selection, the ninth the board had taken, the chairman reiterated the pros and cons of the King James versus the modern, and expected the outcome would be a nondecision, as usual. But without him voting—that in itself a departure—King James went down to defeat.

"Luddy's version," several deacons insisted. And though Luddy had nothing to do with it except to have owned and used some scholar's translation, the new purchase would for a long time be known as "Luddy's Bible."

On a cold February morning, Gilroy and Bessie witnessed the loading of their furniture into the moving van, got in their car, waved to a few well-wishers who had braved the elements, drove to the interstate, and there turned south toward a new life in Florida. The Board of Deacons met the next evening. Not having had in anyone's memory a leader other than Gilroy McAfee—not even a vice-chairman or heir-apparent—they were completely lost.

"We need to elect a new chairman," Luddy said after the impasse had run for an hour, "and then cooperate with him."

Luddy was chosen.

"Hey, fellas," protested Luddy, "I don't know *Robert's Rules* from the Declaration of Independence."

"Maybe not," replied Harry Churtle, "but you got us through the D.R."

He got them through a number of monthly board meetings, too, until the new pastor was called. The Reverend Talbot C. Percival was a take-charge person. He had warned the pulpit committee in his first interview that he held definite opinions—"sanctified convictions" he called them—and brooked no interference in his implementation of divine will. The church was ready for him. Half the members felt that after the ambivalent Peter Barrett, anyone with command in their voice would do. The other half had grown impatient with the upstarts on the board who, despite Luddy's amelioratory efforts, tried running off in all directions. Gilroy McAfee's firm, dignified hand was sorely missed, and perhaps, it was thought, the Reverend Mr. Percival might provide—if lacking dignity and a striving for balance—firmness, at least.

As pastor, Talbot Percival considered himself chairman of the official board, if not in title, in actuality. He allowed no meeting to run more than ninety minutes. He did not approve of Sunday School coming before the morning worship service.

"Some teacher might get wind of my morning message and steal my thunder," he said, and a couple of deacons exchanged winks over words that had been spoken before.

The services were switched around, and if anyone found the restoration inconvenient, not a word of objection was heard.

In approaching the church one Wednesday evening, Luddy saw a cherry picker parked next to the entry tower. Half the shingles on the tapering steeple had been stripped off. Only a few remained that bore the white paint commemorating his slow climb up the spire and his rapid, headfirst descent.

"The contractor will complete the job tomorrow, new shingles and all," explained the Reverend Mr. Percival. "I considered those bespattered shingles an eyesore, hurting our testimony in the community. Replacing them I deemed an emergency, so acted before I could convene the deacons."

Luddy nodded. Yes, of course, it was a good thing to do. He would have asked the deacons to do it, but hadn't known where the money would come from. Evidently, Mr. Percival did. Or maybe that wasn't important.

Reshingling the steeple was a minor matter. Repainting the kitchen wasn't.

The pastor conferred with seven women about an appropriate color and received seven passionate replies that good taste and decency permitted only aquamarine or rose or flaxen or lapis lazuli or some other shade or tint of which he had never heard. He cast aside all opinions and directed his hired painters to spread two coats of white.

"It's so fresh and clean," he proclaimed proudly when the job was done.

White is said to reflect the rays of the entire spectrum. At Rosewood, its scope apparently extended to neither the ray of acceptance nor of contentment.

"I hope that pulpit committee hasn't disbanded yet," said one disenchanted matron at the next meeting of the Ladies Aid. On this, the heads nodding in agreement produced more unity than the group had known in months.

Beulah Simms had little time and less inclination for the ten minutes of study the Aid members engaged in every month, along with five minutes of sentence prayers, fifteen minutes of business, and two hours of fellowship. There were two remaining adult bookstores to be run out of town, and having won prior success, she was sure she and her lieutenants could strike successfully again.

A more liberal City Council had been swept into office, so community standards against pornography were in recent months tempered, making convictions harder to achieve. The police, in fact, turned a deaf ear and a blind eye to the crusading Mrs. Simms and hid behind their thick book of local ordinances every time she called on them to do something. Still, it was illegal to permit minors to buy, browse, or even to set foot inside these establishments.

"I know that as of this moment there are fifteen boys each under the age of fourteen inside the Blue Page Book Shop," she said in a personal visit to Police Headquarters one spring afternoon. Such a charge could not be ignored, so the desk sergeant called the squad car that happened to be nearest the ordinarily quiet, crummy little hole-in-the-wall. Ten minutes later the two officers on the beat reported back. It was true. The place was overrun by young kids. What should they do?

"Throw out all the kids and bring the owner in immediately," their superior ordered.

Mrs. Simms knew that precisely at 4:10 the Blue Page would be infested with an illegal clientele because she had arranged it so with Luddy Newton. At first he had refused to involve his club boys in what he allowed was a commendable effort to re-establish righteousness in the city. But finishing off a generous slab of lemon pie one evening, he wilted under Beulah Simms' motherly eye. He still harbored pangs of guilt for having wronged her nearly two years before when he mistook the presence of girlie magazines on her kitchen counter to be a sign of her personal prurient interest in them. Now he felt he should side with her in this battle, even if his safer self warned against it.

In a special meeting of the club in the church basement one day after school—a day that by driving his helpers uncharacteristically hard he had finished the recycling route early and left the polishing of the truck to them—he outlined the plan he and the Carrie Nation of Pornographic Literature had devised. The boys were to burst into the Blue Page at ten minutes past four, overwhelming the expected protests of the lone clerk and were to stay until the police arrived.

"Will they cart us off to jail?" asked the smallest, most innocent member of the group.

"No," Luddy said, assuring them more than he assured himself. "But they will arrest the bad men who are conducting this bad business."

He instructed the boys to take down no books from the shelves, open no magazines, and to keep moving around the shop. It was the presence of minors that counted. But of course they forgot the details of his instructions and little knots of curious readers gathered in one aisle or another to gawk and giggle at pictures that at this point in their young lives went beyond anything their imaginations had conceived. They might have fulfilled the basic rules of the plan had not on his hurried exit, with one cop yelling for the boys to stand over in one corner and the other for them to leave the building, Will Rankin cradled a magazine in his arms and tossed a dollar bill on the counter, which the proprietor, under the nose of the officers, scooped up and shoved into his pocket.

In the next several hours, that periodical was passed from member to club member. Luddy learned of it only when he was approached by one boy, then another, with questions on certain topics that he found embarrassingly hard to answer.

He would have had another way of learning about Will's purchase, however—the way the readers of the town's newspaper learned of it. A front page story reported that the police found a dozen or more young boys patronizing the adults-only store, and that the charge against the Blue Page's owner, of harboring minors in his shop, was dismissed. What could one man do when rushed by a gang of overactive adolescents who, as it turned out, must have been recruited and coached by a gray-haired grandmother bent on putting him out of a legal business?

It was Will's purchase, completed when the owner stuffed the boy's dollar in his pocket, that padlocked the store for six months.

The baby brought home from the Dominican Republic made the rounds of several Rosewood homes. Her acquired taste for Gerber foods, her outgrowth of infant garments, her panic-causing tears turning suddenly into coos, smiles, and laughter, her colicky nights and slumbering days, and her repeated bouts with croup—these shared experiences brought a number of the church families together in a bond that went beyond their turn at parenting "Luddy's little girl." Eventually, with no family left on the roster to host her, it appeared that Luddy not only would at last get to claim her, as he had wanted to do since his return, but that being her legal parent he probably would be the one to raise her from this day forward.

A single man caring day in and day out for a baby would have found it difficult in the best of circumstances, but Luddy lived in the Young Men's Christian Association, in a tiny room on the third floor. Speaking of the impossible...

Slipping her past the desk clerk the first night was, however, not really difficult.

"I see you've been hiking, Newton," the fellow said in the friendliest of tones as Luddy toted Felicité in a backpack, her head lightly covered with a thin blanket.

"Glad to be home," Luddy replied, without breaking step.

Early the next morning he again strode through the lobby with the pack on his back.

The night clerk was about to yield the desk to the day man, but paused to call to Luddy, "Another hike? You *are* a glutton for punishment."

It wasn't a hike he was to undertake, but a drive to Meribel's.

Getting to this point hadn't been easy. For some time Meribel flinched each time Luddy mentioned the baby's name.

"It's hard to think of her as a mere baby," she'd explain to him.

"Then why don't you get acquainted with her? Hold her, feed her a bottle. She'll grow on you."

She did, when Meribel finally gave her the chance.

For a long time she'd been content to view the baby across the aisle in church, or to glance at her in her playpen or stroller at a friend's house. Babies and Meribel were no combination. Was it her original mistaken concept that blocked acceptance of this particular child, or had she lived so long without infants in her life that to admit one now would require too much rearranging?

Then one Sunday while talking with Meribel in the church vestibule, Ellie Franklin suddenly thrust the baby into her arms.

"Here, hold her a minute. I've got to catch Amy Biddle before she gets away."

To Meribel's surprise, Felicité neither howled nor leaped from her arms. A week later Meribel and Luddy sat with the child while Bob and Ellie went out to celebrate their anniversary. By the end of the evening Meribel was hooked. Now, a new phase of baby-tending was to begin for her.

Luddy bounded up the steps to her porch, toting baby, blankets, and bottles, and at the door handed Felicité over to her. A few days before, she had shifted her hours at Kmart to late afternoon and evening so Felicité would have round-the-clock care—by Meribel during the day, and Luddy evenings and at night. That arrangement had begun.

After a week, the desk clerk at the Y stopped asking about his tenant's penchant for hiking.

Luddy had so practiced the routine of sneaking Felicité in and out through the lobby that when he knew she was a sleepy little papoose in his backpack, he would now and then stop to chat with the desk clerk. One morning she whimpered as he descended the stairs, so there could be nothing but a quick hail as he hurried past the counter.

"Morning, Newton," the night clerk called just as Luddy reached out to push open the door to the street. "The boss said if I saw you I was to tell you he'd like you to stop in at his office."

"I will," said Luddy, opening the door. "First thing I get home this afternoon."

"He's there now. Came in especially before you'd leave this morning."

What was he to do? The boss was Maylan Jackson, general secretary. Among YMCA general secretaries, he was known to run a tight ship. One more step and Luddy would be out of the building and on his way to deliver his charge to Meribel for the day. But no one around the place disobeyed an order or took lightly a request of Maylan Jackson. Yet more convincing to Luddy, someone had asked him to do something, and it was in his nature to do it.

He turned back into the lobby, crossed it, and headed for Jackson's office. His breath came easier when he realized Felicité had settled down under her protective blanket.

"You want to see me, Mr. Jackson?" Luddy said, entering upon Jackson's burst of "Come in!" following Luddy's knock.

"Come in." The general secretary waved him to a chair. "You might want to take the burden off your back. We've got a little talking to do."

"No, I'll keep it on." He eased down into a chair, having room only to rest his haunches on the very front edge.

"Well, just as you wish, Newton. I want you to be at ease. You know we here at the Y constantly try to make our members, especially our resident members like you, feel at home. We're here to help, and that's why I asked you to stop in."

"Oh, this is my home, all right."

"I know... has been for some years now. And from the time we got that matter of illegal meetings of your boys' club cleared away, we've appreciated your stay with us. But there's one item that maybe we can be of help to you."

"I have no complaints."

"Well, let me come to the point."

Luddy felt the baby squirm. He leaned forward to avoid cramping her anymore than a tight-fitting nylon sack stifled a healthy six-month-old infant. Jackson took his movement to be an effort of greater concentration.

"My housekeeper says the maids take three or four diapers from your wastebasket every day. We think maybe you have a problem."

"Me? A problem?"

"And someone on your floor reported to the night clerk they heard crying in your room. We thought perhaps your problem might be worse at night."

"No . . . no." Should he go along with Jackson's assumptions, bear the embarrassment, maybe agree to see a doctor, thank the man for his concern, and then quickly exit? Luddy tried to be honest. On occasion he had shaded the truth—well, not so much fudged it, but left others to draw their own conclusions when he knew they'd draw them in error. But it was always for a higher good. Was there a higher good in breaking the residence rules of the YMCA?

"I've also got a report that you keep milk in the refrigerator of the snack shop."

"Well, yes . . ."

"Not that's there's anything wrong with milk—"

Felicité let out a scream. A pinched finger or arm, or perhaps a toe, had awakened her—or at her tender age, was she so precocious as to recognize the word milk?

"A baby?" Jackson, who had swung his feet upon his desk for this man-to-man talk, suddenly dropped them to the floor, stood up, and peered over Luddy's shoulder. The thin blanket atop the backpack waved in rhythm to the bobbing of a very young and troubled head beneath it. "You carry a baby in that pack of yours?"

"Yeah." Luddy slipped the straps from his shoulders, and whisked off the blanket. Startled at the sudden change in her outlook, Felicité stopped her crying, and seeing two pairs of men's eyes fastened intently on her, turned up her mouth into an enchanting smile.

"A baby... where... whose?"

"Veronica's."

"Why doesn't Veronica have it?"

"She's in the Dominican Republic and Felicité's here with me."

"You and Veronica..."

"I only saw her once."

"I understand."

"No, you don't. You see, I was with the Rosewood Church men last January down in the D.R. and this baby..."

"Yes, those things do happen. I will say it was good of you not to run away without a conscience like a lot of men do."

"She really belongs to the whole team."

"She does? The... whole team?"

"Yeah. All ten."

"Didn't I read in the paper about you men going down there to build something?"

"A school."

"And wasn't our board member Gilroy McAfee—that is, a board member until he moved to Florida—the head of the enterprise?"

"That's right. You never saw a man so tickled as Gibby when he was giving a bottle to our little girl."

"I must say I'm surprised at Gib—at Gilroy. I'm afraid that if the other board members had known—"

"Why, what's the matter with adopting a little helpless orphan?"

"Adopting? Uh... you said you men were down there last January? Let's see, that's six, seven months? That's about how old this baby is."

"Yes, we got her when she was just a couple of weeks old."

"Then I take it she's not yours... I mean, not the child of..."

"I said she was adopted."

Jackson sat down again, trying to be natural in covering his red cheeks with his hands. He wasn't used to playing defensively, so went on the offense.

"We can't allow you to keep a baby in your room."

"If I pay as a double room?"

"There's only a single bed."

"Felicité has her own bed."

"Why have our maids never seen it?"

"When I leave the room in the morning I push it under my bed. The maids never look there."

"That means they don't dust under the bed... let me make a note of that."

"I do her laundry myself, so it's no cost to the Y."

Jackson pulled out a manual from his desk drawer. He quickly leafed through the pages so familiar to him and found the paragraph he wanted.

"It says right here, 'young men of good character. Sometimes we've wondered about you."

"My character?"

"No. Age. On your way to forty—you may be stretching the residence rules a bit."

"But you'll let me keep her for a couple of weeks, until I can make other arrangements?"

"Sorry. No females permitted on the residence floors."

What he should do now, Luddy had no inkling. He trudged up the stairs to his room, retrieved from under the bed the basket he had used as the baby's crib. He laid her in it, then carried the basket downstairs and ignored the dumb-stricken desk clerk as he crossed the lobby to the front door. In the parking lot, he placed Felicité, who once again was asleep, on the back seat of his car and strapped her in securely. He got in, but sat motionless, seeing but not perceiving, hearing, but with no sound registering.

What was he to do now? What was to become of this child? He couldn't expect Meribel to do more than she was doing in caring for her. He felt he had hit bottom. And he'd brought this helpless child down with him. Maybe it would have been better in his fall from the steeple to have hit the ground and died there. Or possibly, it would have been even better if at his dedication as an infant his father had not caught him, but that he'd dropped to the floor and his very young life ended then. He was deep in a depressing mood. Over the last couple of years many good things had happened in his life—so why should this setback floor him? The boys' club; expressing himself to the villagers at Santa María and, important to his teammates, to Señor Mendozo; the opportunity to serve the church as a deacon; reconciliation with Meribel—all this was good. But was it all going for nothing with this present failure?

Why was this baby born? Why was she given to him? Why had God entrusted him with this little life? Why had he allowed him to touch other lives? Him? Luddy Newton? Why him?

Because he was who he was. If the Lord had wanted a Dominican to raise Felicité, would he not have placed her in a Dominican's arms and not his? If another could have saved the men from an unfair prison term, would his tongue have been loosed and his shoulder dislocated while encountering Mendozo on the crest of that mountain road?

Felicité awoke and began a pleasant jabbering in her basket. Luddy inserted the key in the ignition and started his car. He swung out of the parking lot and in the rearview mirror caught a glimpse of the wide grin that had filled his face.

For the first time in his career, Luddy was late to work this morning. He and Meribel had explored a dozen possible solutions to Felicité's problem—really, their problem—and not one of them was practical, nor even possible.

"She'll have to stay here in my house nights as well as days," Meribel finally concluded.

"But you can't keep up your job and get your rest and carry on your life if you're responsible for the baby twenty-four hours a day."

"With your help I can. Other couples do."

"But with you and Felicité here, and me at the Y—"

"Move in here with me."

"Meribel!"

"After we're married, silly."

She ran across the room, threw her arms around him, and passionately kissed him, not once, but several times. He stood immobilized. Then, as if suddenly awakened from deep sleep, grinned his widest at her and walked out the door.

"After we're married..." She'd given him something to think about as he drove off to the recycling center.

Summer gave way to fall with its glorious color and cold weather. Every weekday during these months Luddy went directly from work to Meribel's. Each day Meribel handed him a list of items to feed the baby and things to do for her. He was supposed to put her to bed at seven, but often kept her up beyond eight because during the evening they'd have so much fun romping and playing, or Felicité would be making such good progress in walking that Luddy was hesitant to shut it off. Meribel's shortened hours at Kmart ended at ten thirty and she arrived home before eleven. That meant nearly midnight before Luddy's day ended, though he might have been able to turn in a few minutes earlier if he had not habitually stopped to share with the night clerk Felicité's latest accomplishments.

The pace was wearing on both single parents, so much that in desperation Meribel asked one night before Luddy said "see ya" whether he wanted to get married at Thanksgiving or Christmas.

"Thanksgiving," he said instinctively, thinking more of the "when" question than the "what." He foresaw that the Christmas rush at Kmart would be too much for Meribel to handle if she had to think of wedding plans. So he said Thanksgiving.

The day after Thanksgiving—the county recycling center always closed down on that Friday—Meribel walked down the center aisle of Rosewood Fellowship Church to join Luddy at the altar. In the ceremony straight out of the Reverend Talbot Percival's personally annotated book of pastoral offices, they exchanged their vows, and in the reception line that followed took turns holding a child decked out in a dress that in the eyes of matrons trained in such things rivaled even the bridal gown.

The ceremony was marred by only one mishap—if a procedure thoroughly familiar to the congregation could be labeled that. In receiving the ring from Harry Churtle, his best man, Luddy dropped it and in reaching out to grab it as it rolled under a front pew, dislocated his shoulder. The ring was recaptured, Luddy's windmill rotations reseated the roving joint, Meribel's complexion faded from scarlet to a healthy pink, and the wedding went on to its conclusion.

It was talked about for weeks, not the wedding itself so much, but that after fifteen years more or less, in people's private calculations, the YMCA had lost a resident, Meribel's house had gained one, and in public the couple behaved like amorous, gangling teenagers.

The pastor was glad to have the wedding out of the way. Now, maybe his flock could concentrate on the important elements of parish life, the upcoming election of deacons being one of them. He had engineered a change of the church calendar from a mid-year start to January, so the election was set for the Wednesday night between Christmas and New Year's. Luddy's term was up, and Gilroy McAfee had never been replaced because no one wanted to fill his shoes—probably fearing the comparison between their commonplace ways and his awe-inspiring demeanor. Luddy said he'd prefer not to be nominated again, but the committee ignored his wish. His and Weldon Basker's were the two names presented to the members.

Weldon had kept the job of ushering in the center aisle another year—the fourth by his calculation, the fifth by Bob Franklin's. From the time he and Bob had shared a common misery in the Dominican Republic, held prisoners after the rest of the team departed for home, the feud between them quieted. Thus, Bob made no great fuss when Weldon said he needed one more year to accustom himself to not being chief usher. He'd remind himself each time he passed the offering plates on both sides of the aisle that this time next year he'd be reduced to handling plates from the side aisle for only one section of pews. Given time, psychologically he'd be prepared to hand over the duties and the honor to his associate usher-in-waiting.

Bob said he understood. Since that trip to the Caribbean, he had become a more understanding person. Also, in a very remote corner of his mind, he did some calculating. If Weldon had served as center aisle usher for five years, didn't that set the pattern for his own tenure?

The Reverend Mr. Percival presided at the annual business meeting. "It's not meet that one proposed for election should assume a juridical role." From his seat halfway back in the sanctuary, Luddy said he did not intend to be a candidate, but made no effort to challenge the pastor for the chairmanship, so the session began.

Annual reports from the Ladies Aid, the Young People, the Sunday School, and the Missionary Society were read and approved. The treasurer's report was accepted, even though Sherman Boyer added up the figures in the expenditures column and found an error of two dollars and thirty-eight cents. Then the nominees for deacon were placed before the people. Weldon Basker got up to thank the committee for its faith in him and pledged that if elected he would serve as he had always tried to serve in that most humble of positions, down the center aisle of the church. A slight scattering of applause greeted his remarks. A year ago, before the peace between him and Bob Franklin, he would not have been considered for the official board.

Luddy got to his feet. Standing next to his wife, who gently rocked Felicité in her arms, he swallowed the jawbreaker that he had sucked down to the size of a pea, and began to speak: "I think these jobs should be passed around. I've been a deacon coming up two years now, and there are a lot of men in this church who can take over. Eight that I'm sure of, the eight I went to the Dominican Republic with—nine counting Gilroy McAfee, but I guess we can't count him now that he's moved away. I'm only sorry we're not going back to the D.R. this winter, like we thought we would, but next year—"

"Yeah," called out several men, "Next year."

"If our wives will let us," Luddy continued, and grinned broadly as he put his hand on Meribel's shoulder. She looked up at him.

"You can go. And maybe we women will go along, too."

"For me, it's been an unbelievable two years." He looked down at his wife and child and flashed an even broader grin. "Having a family of my own—"

"Beats the Y, right, Luddy?" called out Sherm Boyer.

"Beats the Y."

He went on to say that he had learned a lot in those deacon meetings under Gilroy McAfee. Building a school—and friendships—in the Dominican Republic was even more of an education.

"I came to realize that if we're willing, even with our unfitness, the Lord will put every one of us to work. I can't really express how I feel. I've never been able to say the things I've wanted to say. My tongue just won't say the words. No, it's more than my tongue. It's me."

"What you *are* did the speaking, Fig," Harry Churtle said in an undertone loud enough to be heard by most folk. "You spoke loud and clear. You were the teacher, and we learned from you."

A wave of assent swept through the assembly.

"Oh, now..."

Luddy started to sink back down in his seat, but stiffened his legs for one last thrust.

"While on my feet, I'd like to nominate Bob Franklin in place of me."

"But I'm an usher, and with Weldon moving to the deacons, I'll—"

"He's an usher now," said Pastor Percival, recovering his wits and his voice, "and if elected deacon, I believe it would be unwise for him to continue as usher."

"Why, pastor?" someone wanted to know.

"The benevolence offering. You know it's taken up at the end of the communion service. It would be unseemly for one who has handled the sacred elements to turn immediately to the mundane."

Before Bob Franklin could object that he had waited five years for the chief ushership, he and Weldon were elected to the board, and the meeting was adjourned. In the unofficial after-session that usually marked these meetings, the pastor said that hereafter there should be two ushers in the center aisle. The duty was too much for one man.

Bob did not feel so bad then, knowing that the singular prize he'd long sought was no longer there. With Luddy's retirement, a chairman of the deacons had yet to be chosen and, well, who could tell...

The Reverend Mr. Percival strongly suggested that Luddy and Harry Churtle be appointed center aisle ushers and Steve Hatfield, instead of Deacon Basker, to work one side aisle. From those who stood around there was unanimous consent.

There seemed to be a lot of unanimity around Rosewood these days.

"Congratulations, Fig," said Harry to his friend.

"Thanks, old buddy. Here, have a jawbreaker." From his pocket he extracted a rather full plastic envelope of big, colorful candy balls. "Everybody have one. They're on me."

The End